I0788712

COOPER Bennett

AND THE DEVIL'S IRE

Cooper Bennett and the Devil's Ire

ISBN 978-1-949584-04-2 (Hardback)

Written by Golden Czermak

Proofed by: Ultra Editing Co.

Illustrated by: Golden Czermak

Cover Design & Photography by: Golden Czermak | FuriousFotog

CONTENT ADVISORY: This is novel contains adult and paranormal themes, coarse language, violence, and some sexual situations.

Even the weak become strong

when they are united.

{Friedrich Schiller}

<u>Dedication</u>

To Mom.

I hope that you're proud.

Love and miss you.

---{-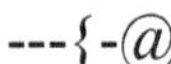

Acknowledgements

Eric, I love you. Thank you for your endless support, even through times where the lights guiding our paths are dim.

Joey Berry, Cooper and his Secret Life would never have been born without our friendship. I'm forever grateful and forever your brother.

Drew Vice, Billy represents so much in these books, qualities and traits that I see within you – beyond the physical resemblance. Thanks for just being who you are and understanding that is a major piece most people fail to realize.

Lovett Taylor, thank you for embodying Grayson and being such a good source of inspiration for him. I can't wait to see where Mr. Manning ends up going in the future, along with our friendship.

Jacob Wilson, my friend, family, OG, and more. My life over the years is better since you're a part of it. I am so happy to see yours is on such a marvelous road.

Brad Arnette, although it's been a long time since we've seen each other, you'll always be the real-life Billy to me.

Kim Tatum, thank you for getting me out of a slump and spurring me to get the words out.

Readers, thank you – all of you – for being there and letting my stories take you new worlds. The level of appreciation that I have for that is immeasurable.

Main Cast of Characters

In alphabetical order by species (pronunciation in parenthesis)

Aves:

Theryn (Therein)

Warryn (Warren)

Bears:

Ásbjörn (Az Born)

Lobjörn (Low Born)

Svarbjörn (Svar Born)

Boars:

Everard

Demons:

Camio

Dajjal (Da Jal)

Wolves:

Alyssa Noble

Billy Arnett

Cooper Bennett

Grayson Manning

Rikolf

Table of Contents

About the Author

In the beginning, Golden worked the standard corporate rat race, completing college with a chemical engineering degree before starting a small photography company on the side.

Since then, the FuriousFotog brand grew into an internationally recognized one, being published in both domestic and international magazines, on websites, and trade/e-book book covers (even appearing on some himself).

Having been in the industry since 2012, Golden has interfaced and networked with countless other authors and clients to create over 600 exclusively licensed book cover images, diversifying into other commercial work as well.

He published his debut novel, Homeward Bound (Journeyman 1) in June 2016, completing the six-book series in January 2017. The rest, as is said, is history.

Websites:

http://www.goldenczermak.com/

http://www.furiousfotog.com/

Other Books by Golden Czermak

FANTASY, PARANORMAL, SCI-FI

The Journeyman Series:

Homeward Bound (Journeyman Series 1)

Seal of Solomon (Journeyman Series 2)

Made to Suffer (Journeyman Series 3)

The Devil's Highway (Journeyman Series 4)

Then Hell Followed (Journeyman Series 5)

Running on Empty (Journeyman Series 6)

Steam Tycoon:

The Steam Tycoon

Cooper Bennett

The Secret Life of Cooper Bennett

Manifest

CONTEMPORARY ROMANCE & EROTICA

The Agency Series:

Cade

The Swole Series:

Swole: Chest Day

Swole: Leg Day

Swole: Wet Wednesday

Swole: Triple Drop Sets

Swole: Flex Friday

Swole: Powerhouse

<u>ANTHOLOGIES</u>

The Frat Chronicles ("The Uncanny Huntsman")

Part One: A Not So Secret Life

Chapter 1

A PRELUDE TO OBJECTS IN MOTION

Friday March 15, 2013

1

With zero Irish roots but plenty of shiny, green plastic to make up for it, the duly good people of Goodman would soon be waking for Saint Patrick's Day festivities. The small Georgia town, nestled in the foothills of the Blue Ridge Mountains, had celebrated the commercialized holiday no less than twenty-seven times since 1985, its streets normally brimming with uncanny leprechauns, synthetic clovers that blanketed the town like some giant had vomited up a glossy salad, and cheesy outfits that tied it all together with bows made from great big gaudy belts.

Yet as fun as those past years were, 2013 would be the twenty-eighth and last time the community (which was no stranger to sinister rumors, dark times, or secret lives) wanted to remember the day. Green would be replaced with red by the gallon when different, deadlier creatures found their way onto the streets, tearing lives apart by jaw and with claw. Werewolves descended upon Goodman – terrifying, vicious, and real.

Fortunately for the townsfolk, their fate was still hours away. It was due after dawn in all its horrific glory, spreading out over the vast forests to the north and east. So, for now, while the people slept in their well-decorated houses under their oversized, cozy comforters, they could dream of pleasant things.

That luxury, fleeting as it was, wasn't the case for others far to the southwest. Wide awake with hearts thumping and lungs taking in gulps of sticky Louisiana air, strange shapes were barreling through the gloom covering the Tensas River National Wildlife Refuge.

"Move it!" a distressed voice urged, and the figure of a man raced forward. An untold number of shadowy *things* trailed behind.

While doing his best to ignore the stinging pain of branches that broke hard against his brow, the streams of blood and surrounding darkness did their best to conceal what lurked at the fringes of his vision. The dim light of an unsympathetic crescent moon was not as kind, shining down between the trees in luminous curtains to show him that nightmares did indeed exist, and that they were closing in.

"Come on, come on!" the man hissed, teeth grinding against each other so tightly they nearly cracked under the pressure of his own words. "You can make it!"

Panic arrived, evicting what little calm tried to stay behind once his eyes locked onto an upcoming copse of trees. It was atop a small embankment, and assuming he was heading in the right direction – the swamp looked the same no matter which way he looked – Parish Road 102 should be waiting just on the other side. From there, a nearby house could allow him to…

A terrible roar cut in, sinking his buoyant thoughts. Whatever bellowed was very close; far too close.

What the hell are those things? a distant voice stirred, his mind demanding answers it surely didn't want to hear.

"Shut up!" The man's fists unfolded, fingers outstretched and trembling like an angry spider. He wiped sweat and blood-ladened grime from his face, transferring it to a dingy white tee shirt. "Not now! We… I… have to focus!"

It was easier said than done (especially when arguing with stray voices in your head). The dense shrubbery undulated as it whizzed by. Dizzying, things started to feel like a prison with a madman beating against the skull walls. He slowed. Then, like the fog that lingered identical to a specter above the tree line, the sounds of heavy footsteps crept in above labored breathing that was not his own.

"No…"

His fists clamped shut, still shaking. His muscular forearms were doing the same.

"No…"

His knees quaked as his pace once again quickened to a sprint. The jeans he wore made swishing sounds that were ominously clock-like, counting down to something grave.

"No!"

The thicket drew closer, his heart lifting with each step. Before long it was beating in his throat, but salvation was just on the other side!

"Yes!"

But his elation proved premature. One of his feet found a patch of soft mud, slipped, then sank deep into the putrid soup. Overbalanced, he toppled, both outstretched palms taking the brunt of an impact against rocks and splinters.

He bit his lip, screaming loudly before sharply cutting off his breath to kill the volume. It was too late. They knew where he was. Maybe they always knew.

There's still a chance we can escape! said the voice in his head.

"Yeah…" the man replied softly. While panting with gentle whispers he decided his remaining strength was better spent pulling himself along rather than arguing.

Crawling toward the road like a snake on its belly, he reached the copse a short time later. From that low vantage point, the gnarled trees rose stoically above him, resembling wizened guardians of some long-lost secret. With their branches pointing in the direction he was headed, things became eerily quiet as he peered around the embankment, and he saw precisely why those sentinels were silent.

There was no road.

No salvation.

No hope.

Instead, even drearier swampland spread out into the darkness like a spongy carpet.

Strength now waning, the dejected man propped himself up on his knees.

Snap.

A sound that could have easily been his bones for all the pain they felt, was instead that of forest debris further breaking under the weight of something huge.

Snap.

It was right upon him, and with barely enough time to catch his breath, the man scrambled behind the closest tree trunk. A low, menacing growl replaced the previous noises. A mere twenty inches or so of wood was the only thing now separating man from nightmarish beast. Though shielded (barely), he felt fully exposed to the world.

We're going to die! his mind blared, and the man didn't have the wherewithal to disagree.

Planting his hands on his temples and his back firmly against the tree, he breathed out deeply and waited on fate.

2

Oh God…

Vibrations started to ripple through the tree. Something was scraping the other side of it, toying with the bark.

Do you feel that? That's going to be our skin next!

"What did I tell you earlier? Stop it!" the man snipped, looking hastily to each side then skyward for any scrap of confidence. "If… no, *when* we get out of this, I'm going to make sure Agares fixes your little talking problem, permanently."

Before the voice could respond, the tremors did. They started to build in both intensity and frequency. In a different time and place, it might have felt relaxing but that night, it was frightening.

The trunk shuddered violently – the way an unwilling victim does when gripped by a seizure – and after a great barrage of noise, the top of the tree was cleaved in a splintering explosion. With all the might of a thunderstorm compressed into a few dramatic seconds, everything was flung outward by the force of the blow.

After landing on his side (which made a cringeworthy *thwack* when it struck the ground), the man was pummeled with shrapnel. Rolling away to protect his face, his nostrils and eyes became caked with warm muck. It blocked his view but a stinging stench lingered, and a faint ringing too.

"How dare you!" cut an astute voice. The tone was bitter, as if the words themselves were insulting to think about and blasphemous to say. "The sheer audacity of a *Journeyman* trying to steal from the glorious House of Tensas. It makes me sick to my stomach!"

"Well, that's where you're mistaken; I'm not part of *that* Order," the man retorted, gaining new confidence (or perhaps stupidity) from the impact. "Besides, the smell of your own breath is probably what's making you sick. I know it's doing the same to me."

Snatched at the collar by a forceful hand, he was flipped like a piece of meat in a hot pan. He gasped, shirt taut against his skin, and when the creature's fingers wrapped around his broad neck, he choked.

"Insolence! Then what did you hope to gain by this?" the thing demanded, and what felt like sharp claws grazed against the human's veins, ripe to puncture. "Power? Notoriety? You will *never* be our equal, human."

"I… wasn't p-p-planning on lowering m-myself to that l-low a level," the captive wheezed, ending with a sly smile wrapped with a stifled laugh. His body jolted abruptly, drawn forward by the beast. "Go on t-then," he pressed, feeling the creature's next words as humid breath on the still clean parts of his skin.

"You'd like that, wouldn't you? You weak, pathetic, little –"

"That's enough Hægen," came another voice. The statement was deep and commanding, its accent laced with a southern twang.

The grip on the man's neck immediately loosened, then was gone.

"Of course, Your Eminence. I meant no disrespect."

Hearing soft footsteps retreating, the man knew better than to run. There was no telling how close any of the creatures were, nor their numbers in the surrounding marshes. Given his failed attempt at reaching the parish road, it was also obvious he had no idea where he was in the basin. The enemy knew that fact, and was sure to take advantage of it.

"Tsk. Tsk," the deep voice continued. It sounded like it was coming from high above. "Did you really think you'd be able to get away, my friend – in completely the wrong direction no less?"

The human felt something padded caress the sides of his face. At first he didn't answer, but the courage to do so unexpectedly arrived seconds later.

"'Friends' isn't necessarily the word I'd use to describe us," he spat.

A chuckle came, and the owner of those same pads began using them to clear the muck from his hostage's face.

Cracking his eyes open – strands of remaining goo still trying to keep them sealed – he saw at once a sight that would make the faintest hearts fail. There was a monstrous creature with dark, shabby fur. Huge and bear-like, two sage-colored eyes stared down at him from nearly a dozen feet off the ground, while cool moonlight mixed with balmy air to make things tenfold more surreal.

"Then perhaps *enemy* suits you far better." The monster placed its left paw squarely in the middle of the captive's chest. Claws out, they easily punctured the thin shirt fabric. "You don't have a single thing to say for yourself?"

When no reply came, its claws inched deeper to help coax out an answer. The man winced, but didn't yield. Instead, muffled growls and low gasps came from the forest.

"You will speak when Lobjörn, the Bear King of the Tensas River Basin addresses you!" Hægen exclaimed from afar.

From what the prisoner could make out when he glanced over in Hægen's direction, he looked like an ordinary man, though quite a frail (and naked) one. Lingering on the embarrassing vision of such a gaunt man tossing him around earlier like a rag doll, the captive managed to hold onto enough confidence to smirk, then state, "That title's quite a mouthful to remember."

Hægen's expression was livid, and he marched forward just as angrily. But the towering beast roared, halting his advance.

Suddenly, there were noises – unsettling and unnatural – that cascaded through the trees. Those green eyes started lowering, not from a simple tilt of the monster's head nor crouching its legs, but because its body was actually collapsing like an accordion without air.

The human watched the thing's limbs groan and pop under the stress of snapping bones, dank hair snaking its way deep into crackling skin. Clumps of muddy residue were left behind, falling away with loud *splats*. Soon the colossus was gone, replaced by a six-foot-three man with broad shoulders and a narrow waist. His left hand still grasping the center of the shirt.

"Then a simpleton such as yourself can just call me 'Your Eminence'," he derided, staring directly into the captive's eyes. "Now, back to the matter at hand. You took something that belongs to me, and I want it back. Now."

The mood shifted as the prisoner, triggered by rage and other forces, found strength enough to push himself forward one tough step at a time.

"No," he answered curtly, the whites of his eyes fading like a light switch had been flipped. Out of the black, his irises blazed with a crimson fire. "You're sadly mistaken if you think the alpha of a lowly shifter species with an equally empty title has the right to own anything of that magnitude. *You're* the simpletons here."

Hægen and the other shifters were stunned into a silent stupor by the revelation. Unfazed, Lobjörn balled up more of the man's shirt in his hand and yanked him closer. Leaning toward an ear with forearm trembling, the shirt started to tear.

"Ah, there you are," he whispered. "I'm not afraid of the Night or its creatures, *demon*, and you'll soon discover that this lowly king's threats are not so empty after all."

"More promises?" the demon snapped. He began to laugh. "That's all you animals ever –"

A mighty blow from the king's right fist ended the conversation early, the possessed body tumbling against the nearby tree. Its trunk buckled, and the demon's body collapsed in a messy heap atop its remains.

"Take that thing back to Big Lake," Lobjörn commanded his subordinates. As they scurried to do his bidding, he opened his fist.

There was a scrap of ripped shirt, which he pinched then cast aside. A silver disc remained in his palm, and two lengths of broken chain dangled from the sides of his hand. Their loose ends danced as if caught by a gentle breeze, and a glimmer of ruby light formed when the ends touched – sealing them together as if they'd never been damaged.

It was then that Lobjörn triumphantly placed the amulet around his neck. He did not know it then – nor would the fact ever sink in past his arrogance – but that mid-March night was one whose consequences would ripple out to lands far from Louisiana, the wild world, and beyond.

Chapter 2

THE NOT-SO-SECRET LIFE OF COOPER BENNETT

Wednesday March 27, 2013

1

The sun is low on the horizon, covered by the mists of morning and a dense cloud of ash kicked up by the marching feet of two advancing armies. One descends from the north by the thousands, creeping like a blight across the land and sky, while another rises to the south, ready to oppose it – not ready to die. Between them all three figures stand; veiled in shadow yet rimmed by light, a small beacon of hope against the oncoming night...

***

A young man named Cooper Bennett flung his eyes open, still reeling from his most recent dream (one of many that had been plaguing him with strange visions since the town's grotesque incident a couple of weeks earlier). Befuddled, he failed to judge the distance to the low branches of the tree he'd picked to sleep under, and as he sat bolt upright with an unbruised forehead rushing toward the lowest branch…

"Ouch!"

Perhaps it was the *thump* that woke Cooper's girlfriend Alyssa Noble from her restful nap in their secluded hideaway along Wolf's Ridge Greenway, or the loudness of his yelp, or (most likely) the string of profanity that was spilling out of his mouth.

"Cooper?" Alyssa asked with concern, seeing him rolling around like a flea-ridden dog in a pair of dirty boots, ripped jeans, and a white wife-beater beside her. It looked hilarious (his hair was a messy, black mop by then), and while trying to hide her beaming grin things turned serious once she noticed the large contusion taking shape on his forehead. "Coop, are you okay?"

Things would have remained that way if not for the immediately crazed look he gave her. Troubled, austere, and downright cute all at the same time, it sent her defenses crashing into a fit of laughter before he even had a chance to say "yes" or otherwise.

"Gee, thanks for the concern, baby," Cooper said sarcastically (Alyssa still laughing). "It's a good thing you love me, eh?" Slowly working his way back up into a sitting position, he rubbed on the bruise. It stung, but only slightly.

"I guess I like you *somewhat*," she replied casually, now examining the wound herself. Gently patting its outside edge with her fingertips, to Alyssa's surprise (or rather what *should* have been surprise if she didn't already know Cooper's secret), the black and blue coloring was already receding.

"Mhmm, sure," he replied, wincing before taking the opportunity to steal a look at her beautiful blue eyes. The afternoon sun tumbled through the spring leaves, its warmth twinkling in them. It made him happy. He also saw her eyes flash faintly green from time to time as she studied the healing bruise. His eyes did too as he gazed back at her.

Those shimmers weren't a trick of the light; Cooper Bennett happened to be a werewolf, you see, or rather a wolf shifter if one needed to be that technical about it. Although he wasn't like the ones who'd attacked the town, Cooper had been affected by them nonetheless, literally dragged into his new life the prior year one fateful night in Toluca Springs. Over the next seven months, he'd discovered that being a shifter wasn't like the old monster B movies he'd enjoyed from time to time with his best friend Billy Arnett – bad makeup jobs and cheap costumes that were right at home at the less publicized bottom of a double feature poster. Those were pure fantasy. No, in reality shifters were very fast and frightening, and the burden their presence brought to those affected was an emotionally heavy and cruel toll.

Goodman itself had discovered the cost first-hand just eleven short days earlier, and even though the Order and its alliance of human and supernatural beings raced in to restore normality like it did every day across the globe, horrific experiences like that did not like to be ignored nor covered up like dust swept under a decorative rug. Often they persisted deep in memory, with lasting (and irreparable) damage. The pressure boiling under the artificial veneer constructed by the Order would have to be unleashed one day – voluntarily or not.

But Cooper didn't want to think about any of that while awake, his dreams doing their best to remain an ongoing and unwanted reminder. Yet every time he would see Alyssa going forward – unassuming in her crop top, snug jeans, beaded headband, and boots – he would have to. She was also a shifter, sealing her own fate about an hour earlier with a well-timed lip bite when they kissed.

"It's gone," Alyssa said.

"I know, and I wish you hadn't done it," Cooper muttered. He laid back on the grass, for a split second thinking she was on the same wavelength as he was – talking about her former life.

She wasn't.

"Done… what, exactly? I thought it didn't hurt."

"Huh?"

"The bruise, Coop, *it's* gone," Alyssa clarified. "Wait. What did you think I was referring to?"

"Oh… nothing," Cooper shrugged off.

"Cooper!"

Childishly, he threw an arm over his face to block Alyssa's intense stare, but felt her nestle against his side nonetheless. Repositioning himself at once, she used Cooper's upper arm as a makeshift pillow while he played with her long, blonde hair.

He felt so conflicted; it was Cooper's selfishness that wanted to keep her near (close like they were now, so he would never have to let her go), but it was his true love for her that wanted (and needed) her to be out of reach, since there was no doubt danger would flock to him like a moth to a flame.

"I was talking about your… decision," Cooper continued reluctantly.

"I thought we went over this."

"Briefly, for sure, but this muddle of a puddle runs far deeper than that."

"I know." Alyssa smiled instinctively, those annoying Cooper-catch-phrases like little bursts of joy. "We'll tackle those issues – all of them – together as intended."

"But you had a promising future away from this godforsaken town," Cooper stressed. "Away from all the craziness. Away from me…"

"Most of my life, to this point at least, was spent being what others wanted me to be, or what I thought they would want to make my life easier."

"Like that one beaver-toothed chick?" Cooper snapped his fingers several times in thought. "Vivian I think?"

"*Virginia*," Alyssa giggled, "and her cronies."

"Yep, I remember them," Cooper said with a final, endorsing finger snap.

"I couldn't be myself," Alyssa continued, "Liam making sure that his little cheerleader stayed in the lane he dictated." Her voice trailed off, the hurt that the memory of Liam's recent passing was still substantial despite their history. "That last point – being away from you, Cooper Bennett – is why I couldn't leave, and it's a fact that hasn't changed."

"You say that now, Alyssa, but time's been far too short and…"

"And I'll say it again tomorrow, Cooper."

There was a finality in her voice that Cooper didn't want to challenge. Surely that would spark an argument. Instead, they both grew silent, a few seconds passing before either said another word. It was Alyssa who did first.

"Come on," she urged peaceably, "enough of that topic for now. There'll be plenty of time to talk about it later. Let's just have a little "us" time before things pick up again."

Cooper sighed in agreement, knowing things would indeed pick up soon. The two settled into each other's arms, and though Alyssa seemed to have no trouble falling asleep again, Cooper's mind didn't want to slow down.

He mulled over many subjects, and after succeeding in pushing most of that to the side, he watched a couple of butterflies flitting overhead. Their blue wings looked like soft flower petals against a field of green leaves.

Caterpillars are forced to change, Cooper thought, *and they make out alright, able to take flight afterwards.* He then wondered if her hair would get thicker and darker like his did. While teasing hers between his fingers, he was sure that it would still be as stunning as the day his eight-year-old eyes first saw her alone on the steps of Riverhill School.

Cooper would be lying if he told anyone – especially himself – that he wasn't worried about her transformation, though it wasn't so much the physical ones he had issues with. After all, he had changed for the better over that time.

It was the other aspects of the Change, the things that he didn't like to talk or even think about, that scared him.

Hunger…

Meat...

Blood...

2

Still awake after half an hour, Cooper knew that sleep wasn't coming anytime soon. Ever since being bitten up in the mountains at the end of August 2012 by a black wolf, and within a day seeing those severe wounds healing right before his eyes (and without the glasses he'd worn for over a decade), he knew that he wasn't going to be normal anymore.

With the path of being a shifter laid out before him, and with the imminent threat that was Lance Goddard – Alpha of the Shadow Wolves – now gone, he had to walk that trail, picking up the pieces of his life that were left messily behind.

He missed aspects of an ordinary life, like eating carefree breakfasts, lunches, and dinners – even in the simplest or most judgmental homes. He missed Goodman High School; not so much the unsightly red-bricked building, classes, or teachers (Mrs. Sanderson and her trademarked stare for one), but the time with friends and their growing relationships. Besides, he'd asked Alyssa to go to the prom with him all the way back in the fall, and due to circumstances beyond any of their control, those plans were now cancelled. He missed those future times the three of them – Alyssa, Billy, and Cooper; the ABCs – would have together, because no matter what, things were going to be different now, even more so than if they'd just graduated and went on to respective campuses or careers.

What he didn't miss was his, or rather his father Roland Bennett's house on Hanscom Road, with its thinly furnished interior, leaky roof, and musty stench permeating every room, including his meager bedroom that was so sparse it didn't even have a mattress – only three tatty sheets that he would use for bedding. Along those lines, Cooper thought he would actually miss his father, but found that Roland's demise didn't leave a gaping hole in Cooper's life.

At least I don't have to worry about belt marks anymore, Cooper thought positively.

How ironic that Roland named his own son after a dog, who became a werewolf, whose kinsfolk slayed him nineteen summers later. That trail of thought brought Cooper back to worrying about where things would go, especially taking on the mantle of Shadow Alpha in place of Lance. Those creatures – the same things that rampaged through his hometown and ended so many lives – would now be under his control. That left a bitter taste in his mouth and made the decision to be their Alpha all the more difficult to swallow.

Part of him, chiefly Cooper's heart, hurt at the injuries his friends sustained during the attack, none more than Billy Arnett. His stout buddy, who took on the might of the Gray Mother – first of all werewolves – himself, saved the day but with the cost of losing his right leg and his wonderful parents. He was recuperating in

Goodman Hospital, Alyssa and Cooper planning to visit him later that night. Cooper didn't know how Billy would respond to the Change, a bite from the Mother of All Werewolves territory not something that happened often, if ever before. Frightening to think about, and of course the mental outcome was always the worst, Cooper also missed the Arnetts profoundly, wondering how they would handle their boy's transformation. Would they even know about it, would Billy be able to live out a secret life himself, or would things have gone south, with Billy changing and the hunger arriving? Cooper didn't want to think about it, locking that series of thoughts away in a mental box and throwing away the key.

What Cooper realized as he rid his mind of the oppressing negativity was all the worry didn't matter. Regardless of what he wanted, obtained, or was denied, life would continue to march on. Cooper understood that he didn't need to flee Goodman or the Blue Ridge Mountains any longer, since he could be happy anywhere with the people he cared about.

Would they want to stay around you as much as you do them?

His mind was always playing devil's advocate and, honestly, Cooper didn't know the answer to its question. Time would tell, revealing all secrets and motives in due course. He just needed to have the patience to ride out the journey and enjoy the time on it, even if the destination wasn't where he wanted to be. But right then, he was exactly where he needed to be – beside Alyssa as restful thoughts, the warm sun, and forest sounds enticed him to sleep at last.

35

Chapter 3

A DIRE SITUATION

1

Alyssa and Cooper woke up a couple of hours later; the air was cooling down, sky tinted a purply-orange as the sun shifted further west. Alyssa had been first to wake, the slumbering wolf-boy about ten minutes later.

Cooper stretched, yawned deeply (and quite noisily), then glanced over in her direction. "Woah!" he yelled, caught off guard by Alyssa's wide stare mere inches from his face.

"Really?" she said, flabbergasted, slapping an open palm against his chest.

"Well, I wasn't expecting you to be that close! What were you staring at anyway?"

"A spider!" Alyssa exclaimed. "It was a big one too, about to crawl right up your nose!" She looked around anxiously. "In fact, I think it did!"

Cooper laughed nervously, his expression saying *surely she's just joking*. Swiping the base of his nostrils a few times just for good measure, nerves got the better of him (Alyssa's look hadn't changed from frantic), and he shoved a finger right in there to coax the bug out. With the force he used, he might have pushed it into his brain.

"It was the *other* nose hole," Alyssa corrected, her tone far-too-serious.

Cooper had already started to switch sides, cocking an eyebrow when she burst with glee.

"Glad you think me giving myself brain damage is hilarious," he groused.

"You're right," she said, "though all those boogers should have made a soft impact."

Cooper sat up, rolled his eyes, then chuckled.

"Seriously though," Alyssa said, "I was just admiring that face is all."

"Dashing, isn't it?" Cooper responded, stroking the scruff of his beard with the hand that wasn't mining for nose gold. He noticed her hair seemed a touch darker in the shade than before.

"It is," she replied simply, "but nowhere near as good at what's on the inside."

Cooper thought about retorting with another booger line, but leaned toward her instead. He kissed Alyssa's cheek, then with a hand on her chin guided her lips over to his.

Muffled, Alyssa started to ask, "That's not the same hand that…" but Cooper cut across her with a quick (and untrue), "No."

2

Even though the downtown square of Goodman suffered the brunt of the blow dealt by Lance and his pack of Shadow Wolves, Castillo's Pizza managed to endure as the one bright, greasy spot in the area. The ABCs had made the place their hangout, and most of the other stores along Market Street were closed, so it seemed appropriate to Cooper and Alyssa that they should head that way for a bite to eat before traveling further west to the hospital.

The inside of the Italian eatery was still quaint, though the number of customers was decidedly low, even for a weekday. As Luciano Pavarotti sung *Nessun Dorma* over quiet speakers, Cooper couldn't help but wonder how many people would never be back, either from moving away, post-traumatic stress, or worse fates. He looked around, the cream and maroon walls that originally reminded him of Parmigiano-Reggiano and Bolognese now hinting at fouler things, while aromas from the kitchen did their best to suppress those revolting thoughts under mounds of spaghetti, calzones, and tiramisu.

Seated at their favorite spot – the middle set of several booths lining the now smudged windows that bordered Hanlon Road – Cooper stabbed the tines of his fork into his Veal Milanese. It seemed strange to be there without Billy, whose antics would have provided a good source of cheerfulness and enjoyment that was much needed now.

"Should we get him something?" Alyssa asked, taking a bite of branzino. She knew Cooper's thoughts were on Billy; hers were too.

Cooper looked up from his plate, then briefly across the street to the shuttered exterior of Kimmy's Donuts. The place, which used to bustle with customers and shine with glazed donuts like gemstones of every color, stood dark, depressing, and empty.

"Coop?"

He didn't answer.

"Cooper?" Alyssa repeated a touch louder.

He finally looked her way, eyes misty.

"He'll be okay," she told him. She set down her fork, grabbed his hand. Her thumb rubbed him gently.

"Um, yeah," Cooper said somberly. A sniffle followed. "We should get him some mozzarella sticks for when he wakes up. He loves those and will definitely be…" Cooper's voice trailed off before the last word emerged. "… hungry."

"He likes those way too much," Alyssa agreed, obviously trying not to think about exactly what Billy would be hungry for.

Flagging down the waiter, a handsome man named Matteo returned to their table once he'd refilled a glass of water for a customer at one of the central square tables. When being seated earlier, Matteo – who was a new face to both Cooper and Alyssa – had told her that he was there to help his relatives Piero and Adriana Castillo work through the physical and emotional damage they'd sustained. Jotting down Alyssa's order (she'd added some biscotti for good measure) he nodded gracefully, smiled charmingly, then glided over to a nearby couple – the only other people in the place.

"Ol' Italy sure did seem super excited to come talk to you again," Cooper pointed out offhandedly.

"You really have to stop," Alyssa said. "You've nothing to worry about, Mr. Alpha. Although, now that you mentioned it, Matteo *is* quite charming. I mean that accent… whew!"

"One wet floor sign for Miss Noble, please!" Cooper said, eyes rolling as Alyssa pretended to fan herself. Moments later, he noticed the time on a wall clock opposite them. "Once we get Billy's food we should get going. It'll be sunset by the time we arrive at the hospital, and I want to be sure we have plenty of time to prepare."

"Do you think this is going to be bad?" Alyssa asked, quashing a gulp.

"I have no idea," Cooper said truthfully, "and it scares me, right to the core."

3

Cooper looked around the sterile hospital room, perched at the edge of one of the stiff and scratchy guest chairs (which Goodman Hospital had spared no expense on the purchase of, literally). The walls were monochrome except for the odd pops of color from blinking lights and glowing displays, stripped of any liveliness by the antiseptic smell that filled the air.

Heaven forbid anyone be allowed to be cheerful in here, Cooper thought, thankful to have a different perspective than last time. He still hated being in the room, reminded of that past September when he was being treated for that accursed wolf bite.

To his left, Alyssa was sitting with her arms crossed, fast asleep again.

What aren't you telling me, baby? he wondered and worried. With the excessive fatigue, he hoped she was telling him everything, and that the Change wasn't having some kind of ill effect on her.

To his right was a trivial table near the door. Where he could recall modest cards, small gifts, and food on his when he was an inpatient, the only things there for Billy were a get well soon card from the two of them and the boxed food from Castillo's. Cooper felt bad there wasn't more – things like a pie from Mrs. Arnett or even a huge bag of gummi bears from Schneck's Grocery uptown.

I wish there was more buddy; you deserve it.

That left the view ahead of Cooper, which he tried his best to avoid, yet was the entire reason they were there. Difficult and sad to see, Billy laid in the hospital bed. Unconscious and there for the past eleven days, he had been covered by a blue and white speckled blanket, beneath which he wore a gown. The exposed parts of his arms, neck, and face still bore terrible scratches and bruises – the worst hidden beneath all the fabric. On the right side of his body, the blanket dropped away suddenly below the knee. There was nothing there anymore, and Cooper was left with the vision of that hunk of meat digesting slowly in the drowned stomach of the Gray Mother, trapped where they'd left her in the flooding Order Vault that sprawled beneath the town.

Head in hands and tears ready to flow, Cooper tried his best to find some humor, any at all, in what he saw. He noticed the catheter bag hanging off the side of the bed, remembered Alyssa telling him Billy and her had watched him fill it several times the weekend he was there, yet it didn't do anything for him. No laughter came, only sorrow.

Billy... I'm so sorry Billy.

Cooper wept, then when he thought he was finished, wept more. Standing, he began to rock with arms crossed.

Bee-beep.

Pacing around the room, Cooper clasped his hands together as a stress headache started forming.

Bee-beep.

The noise from the monitors wasn't helping, Cooper now rubbing the corner of his eyes and the bridge of his nose to alleviate some of the pressure.

Bee-beep.

Anything to try and pacify that prickly, unsettled feeling.

Bee-beep.

Exhaling deeply, he looked out the narrow windows. The Venetian blinds were opened just enough to see the light of a full moon spilling onto the parking lot outside.

"Well, buddy, it's almost time," Cooper said, sputtering. "I hope Dr. Ross has you pumped up with enough drugs, otherwise this is going to be quite a shit show..."

4

"Well, we'll find out tonight actually," Cooper mentions as they walk beside the creek. "There's a full moon, and if he's not in a medically induced sleep, we should be there for him should anything happen."

"We should go regardless," Alyssa says, holding Cooper tightly.

***

Cooper's earlier conversation with Alyssa while at Wolf's Ridge Greenway resonated in his mind. He approached Billy warily, observing all the hoses, wires, and other devices attached to his friend's damaged body. Billy looked harmless enough, just like he was sleeping (except there was no excessive snoring), but if life had taught Cooper anything over the last year, it was that things were never what they appeared to be.

Cooper noticed Billy's hair was darker in patches, nearly black in some longer strands that curled just above his eyebrows.

That's just a physical change, Cooper alleged to soothe himself. *It doesn't mean anything evil's happening, but is Billy's build already bigger too?*

Surely not. Cooper's anxious mind was just playing tricks on him. It took Cooper nearly a month to show that much of a bodily transformation in his human form, and Billy still had cuts and scrapes everywhere – something Cooper healed from in days. The contradictions were strange. Cooper stepped closer to get a better look. Crouched down.

Billy had always been a stout, meat and potatoes kind of guy, but he was definitely larger now, with a smattering of body hair and a light beard.

Cooper couldn't remember all the medical-speak that Dr. Ross told him was happening on the inside, but even with the variations there was no denying what he saw, and Cooper swallowed hard.

This has to be due to the bite coming from the Gray Mother instead of some regular wolf, Cooper mused.

Alyssa mumbled from her makeshift bed near the windows, somehow still sleeping upright in that abomination masquerading as a chair. Alarmed, Cooper shot a look that way, but once he saw her napping quietly, he dropped his guard and started to smile. That moment is precisely when the unexpected came, as should have been expected.

The next moments were a whirlwind of terror, sweat, and blood. It lasted seconds but felt like an eternity.

Heart rate monitors beeped feverishly, their chirping rising fast before crashing to a flatline.

"Billy!" Cooper darted toward him, grabbing his friend at the chest by the gown. "Billy are you alright?"

There was sweat on Billy's forehead, lots of it, and the drone of no beating heart was like a knife to Cooper's own.

"Billy!" There was no answer, Cooper crying as he pressed his lips to Billy's cheek. "No… this can't be… no…"

Bee-beep.

Cooper didn't hear the heartbeat return, nor see Billy's eyes as they opened; a deep red glaze coating his once tender stare. It was only when Cooper felt Billy's tight hands around his neck that he realized what was going on, and that it was evil indeed.

Billy's hold was strong. It kept Cooper locked in place, slowly bringing his cheek toward Billy's mouth.

"Meat…" Billy mumbled, the sound detached and icy. "Fresh…"

Cooper pressed hard against Billy's chest, lifting his head away. He managed to move, but not enough, Billy's hot breath wafting over and sharp teeth cutting into Cooper's skin. He felt searing pain, blood gushing down to the clean bedding. There was chomping, and slurping; the sounds of gluttonous feasting were unavoidable.

"Sorry, buddy," Cooper managed to say, and as his eyes gleamed like an emerald in the sun, black and white hair streamed from his mangled body.

Cooper's clothes were torn and fell away as he escaped Billy's hold, his wolf-like body crashing into the chair he'd been sitting on earlier. It broke beneath his four monstrous legs as he rebalanced, the front two then breaking with a chilling *snap*, reforming into long, arm-like limbs. Sharp claws emerged from the ends of his fingers, and he stood up tall, ready to defend himself.

"Billy…" Cooper snarled, the monster's voice croaking severely. "Don't… do… this. Stop… It's me…"

Billy was still in the bed, the last part of Cooper's flesh being chewed so incredibly slowly, then swallowed. "More," he said, crazed and with no intention of stopping nor any idea who Cooper was. Standing slowly on the thin mattress, blood all around and somehow balancing on one leg, Billy also began to change. His body grew, sinewy and muscled; ragged hair the color of rust rending the gown as it erupted from his pores. The bed buckled under his rising weight, and the creature let out a roar that shook the building itself.

"Oh boy…" Cooper growled. Billy's form was at least twice the size he was normally. Fully aware that shifters weren't shackled to the whims of the moon and that the first full one initiated the Change, Cooper wasn't prepared to fight something *that* big.

Billy didn't give Cooper any more time to think. He rushed straight at him, fast, and Cooper dodged then swiped in the nick of time. Both beasts clashed right there in that small town hospital room off Market Street. The noise was intense. Walls cracked. Skin ripped. Lights shattered. Jaws bit.

"Billy… come on bud," Cooper howled hopefully. "I know you're in there!"

Billy responded with a dominant bite to Cooper's shoulder. More agony.

Scowling, Cooper slashed at Billy's left leg to take him down, realizing the right one (the missing one) had fully regrown.

In that moment of distraction, Billy grabbed, lifted, and threw Cooper toward the entrance. His body smashed against the door, jamming it in the frame.

Cooper tried to stand, toppling into the debris. Pain coursed through every inch of his body in throbbing fits.

Billy approached regardless, drool cascading from his jaws to the tile floor like a red rain.

Splat.

The edges of Billy's mouth turned upward into a wicked smile. The hunger had taken hold. Cooper could see himself from the night he first changed, and the vagrant whose life he ended reflected clearly in Billy's wanton eyes.

Splat.

Billy loomed above, head bobbing freakishly.

"If this is my penance for what I did," said Cooper ruefully, his eyes closed. "So be it."

A specter of death now come for its payment, Billy's jaws opened wide, and he lunged forward to finish that delicious first meal.

Chomp!

It was an awful sound, but there was no pain. Unexpectedly, Cooper heard another roar. It was filled with woe.

Opening his eyes, he saw that it was coming from Billy. Another wolf – its fur dark like a moonless night and eyes the color of jade – had latched firmly onto Billy's back. Its powerful mouth was clamped shut on his left shoulder, Billy trying his best to tear it off.

"Alyssa?" Cooper barked with astonished horror. He leapt to action. "Alyssa!"

Reaching backwards, Billy managed to grab hold of Alyssa by the nape of her neck. He squeezed, hard. There was a definite *crack.*

Then she yelped, her whines stinging Cooper's ears.

Billy threw her body wholly to the ground like a piece of trash.

Alyssa struck hard, rolled, then stopped against a nearby cabinet. An IV stand and other equipment toppled around her. She was dazed.

Billy stepped forward, then again. One of his massive, clawed feet was raised and ready to snuff her out.

"Owooooo!" Cooper howled, striking Billy hard. The two wolves fought, breaking through the wall into the adjacent room.

Cooper didn't know if it was occupied or not – he hoped it wasn't – but there was little time to dwell on it. His full focus was on Billy, struggling to bring his beastly friend back from the brink.

The two engaged again, thunderous. The ensuing fight was brutal, the two rooms reduced to rubble, their bodies the same.

There was a loud *thud*. Cooper flew through the air, hurtling into the bed. Shaking off the impact, he looked toward the hole in the wall, filled with a slobbering behemoth that was once sweet, innocent Billy Arnett.

It's got to be you or me, Cooper realized, and standing with the last of his strength he accepted that choice.

Beneath his feet, the hospital blanket fluttered like a dying blue and white butterfly, stomped by a ruthless child. Yet Cooper should have remembered that no matter how dire a situation could be, when the three of them were together there was always hope. No matter how small a glimmer…

Alyssa hobbled between the two of them – back to Cooper, her long face forward to Billy. Cooper could not see it at the time, but she had a chain hanging from her mouth. At the end of it dangled a white ring; a gift from Billy's late father, Branson. It glinted in the flickering fluorescent light, and Billy gazed toward it.

Cooper had another ring (well, it was somewhere in the rubble at least), the pair of them representing his brotherly love and family bond with Billy.

Alyssa said nothing as she stood, the intensity behind her stare enough. She looked confident and strong, but Cooper suspected she was just as suspicious and anxious as he was on the inside. Billy's next move would determine if their relationship ended in ruin, or would continue from it.

The beast took a step forward, groaning.

Cooper stiffened, but saw a look in Billy's eyes. There was alarm and pity there, showing through flecks of his natural color that had returned.

The behemoth then fell to his knees, a low howl leaching out and over the sounds of destruction around them.

Relief washed over Cooper. He took a step, rested a hand on Alyssa's neck, and rubbed. It was over for now, and the trio would have a lot of time to –

Boom!

The door to Billy's hospital room abruptly burst open, a large-framed man pushing his way through the damage. It was Dr. Wen Ross, and as he surveyed both rooms (since there was now a pass-through) he wore disbelief on his face.

Stopping to examine the three massive creatures taking up the center of the wrecked room, he folded his arms across his broad chest like a father would for a disobedient child. He should have been scared, but he had seen this sort of thing several times before, though never in that amount of up-close detail. Regarding Cooper, then Alyssa, then Billy in turn, Dr. Ross had to do a double take with Alyssa, then a triple with Billy.

"Mr. Bennett. So nice to see you," Dr. Ross said without much pleasantry. "It seems that we have a lot to catch up on, and you have a lot of explaining to do. I mean, how in the *hell* am I going to explain this to the Committee?"

One of the overhead lights sputtered, then detonated in a shower of sparks and broken glass.

Cooper let out a muted howl. "Gas… leak?" he growled, and Dr. Ross had no choice but to laugh.

"It *is* really good to see you again, Cooper," Dr. Ross said. "Now, let's get you three, um, changed. 'Gas leaks' of this magnitude have a ton of paperwork, so we better get started."

Chapter 4

THE GREAT BEAR KINGDOMS OF LOUISIANA

Friday May 22, 1863

1

Brashear City sat on the banks of the Atchafalaya River like it had since the days it was known as Tiger Island. Ironically, the wild cats of the area that inspired surveyors to give it that original name were rather ordinary when compared to some of the territory's more diverse and interesting inhabitants; namely bear shifters that had taken hold in the region.

The settlement had sprung up, as its motto from future years would state: "right in the middle of everywhere," roughly the same distance from Baton Rouge to the north, Lafayette to the west, and New Orleans to the east.

The presence of bear shifters in the region was elusive, the Order mindful of their arrival since the early Sixteenth Century. The species came in small numbers alongside European (mainly Spanish) explorers at the time, taking to the forests and marshes before humans returned to develop the area more than a century later. With a foothold on the land, similar to other shifter populations around the country, they were able to have an upper hand, and live in relative peace.

That is, until war came upon them nonetheless. However, there was no combat between shifters and humans, rather a civil war had been brewing between the humans themselves for some time, finally spilling over to consume them all.

The fight – which was splitting a nation – arrived on the bear's doorstep, and the disparate clans were forced to unite under a single banner to survive. Svarbjörn, Alpha of the Atchafalaya River Basin, had edged out another to claim the new and rightful title of Bear King.

It was the second half of May, and a lengthy military siege of Port Hudson by Federal forces had just begun. They had eyed the settlement, seeking control of the main nautical thoroughfare through the region: the Mississippi River. Taking the Port would undoubtedly lend itself to that goal, allowing the Federal army to dominate the region.

In turn, the Confederates devised a plan to counter the Federal army and divert their attention away from the Port. An attack was strategized for the Lafourche district – a region of lower Louisiana to the south and west of the Mississippi River; it housed the parishes of Assumption, Lafourche, and Terrebonne. Occupied by Federal forces for the last seven months, many of their troops were being sent to Port Hudson for the siege. If the Lafourche district could be taken back into Confederate hands, they could then use that leverage to threaten New Orleans itself, forcing the Federal army to move away from Port Hudson in order to protect the city.

Part of the two-pronged effort was seizing control of Brashear City, and in June the Confederates launched their assault by way of the Teche Bayou, helped by some very unexpected – and very large – allies. Colonel James P. Major lead a Texas cavalry brigade, supported by Svarbjörn's Defenders of the Realm, to cut off the Federal retreat by blocking the west bank of the Mississippi. The site of horses and bears storming the countryside must have been a strange sight to behold.

To further ensure the Federal army's attention was drawn away from Brashear City, the second part of the attack was implemented. A small detachment of cavalry and bears attacked a Federal position at Lafourche Crossing, that skirmish ending in a Federal victory. Despite the losses, it served the Confederates well enough, keeping the enemy from reinforcing Brashear City until it was successfully captured on the twenty-fourth of June, along with ample Federal supplies.

All seemed good, but in the aftermath of the conflict things soured quickly. Strife that had been brewing within the Bear Kingdom broke loose, steered by a former Alpha named Lobjörn, and a shifter civil war was poised to erupt before the bodies of their brethren were even cold.

2

Sunday March 31, 2013

The seven o'clock sun rose over St. Mary Parish, Svarbjörn standing alone on the north side of Bayou Boeuf that morning. In his human form, he was an incredibly large man, as wide as he was tall, covered with a forest of body hair. The breeze was already warm and would only get hotter as the day went on, the King positive that the conversations he would have within the hour would be just as heated.

"What exactly are you up to Lobjörn?" Svarbjörn asked aloud, his Cajun accent heavy like the shrugging shoulders that stretched the limits of the motorcycle club vest he wore.

There had always been tensions between the two kingdoms – arising from their rough formation, but nothing had ever threatened to throw things out of balance. That is, until that past February, when something changed and threatened to collapse the entire region. Lobjörn had done a lot of saber-rattling since the civil war, but his efforts had shifted into high gear and he now looked ready to crash into anything that got in his way.

Turning away from the vibrant green trees across the gleaming orange water, Svarbjörn lumbered across a salvage yard, used marine equipment and recovered vessels to his sides. In contrast to his surroundings, a brand new Harley-Davidson Fat Boy was waiting ahead, parked on a patch of loose gravel. Straddling it, massive legs straining, he donned a helmet then pulled the clutch lever. Starting her up, a deep rumble indicated that she was ready to ride, and Svarbjörn, being the good king that he was, didn't want to keep his subjects waiting.

He rode out, past the levee walls, and onto 2nd Street, turning left on Federal Avenue toward the clubhouse. It was a couple of miles north. As he passed by small wood-sided homes that transitioned to equally small businesses, his thoughts fell back on his counterpart-turned-nemesis, Lobjörn, and his destructive effects on the community the Bear King had grown to care for – even love.

"I hope you can see reason, before you do something we all cannot recover from." Svarbjörn's muttering was quiet but hopeful, yet something told him that Lobjörn would not see reason.

Federal Avenue abruptly came to an end, intersecting with Levee Road. Svarbjörn made a right turn, then an immediate left, pulling into the clubhouse parking lot a few seconds later. There were times that the outside of the brick building was lined with over a dozen bikes. Sunlight, neon lights, and, at times, both would glimmer across their chrome trim and glossy paint. This was not one of those times, the lot completely empty except for a single '78 Triumph Bonneville.

Svarbjörn had wanted it that way in case things went south. Stepping off the bike, he removed his helmet and hung it on the closest handlebar. Walking to the main entrance (a chunky, weather-beaten sheet of metal) he sighed, grabbed the handle, and pushed his way inside.

3

Svarbjörn entered the small foyer, a cracked light fixture overhead carpeted by dead moths. It cast a jaundiced tint on his skin as he passed through to a larger room. The interior was melancholy; the normally robust smells of cigar smoke, beer, and musk from dozens of bear-men who would be seated around the various sofas and chairs were low-key. Ella Fitzgerald was singing quietly from a glowing jukebox in the corner, reminding the Bear King that *Into Each Life Some Rain Must Fall.* Sadly, he knew all about that first hand, and agreed.

Ahead was a bar, the centerpiece of the establishment with amber bottles of bourbon and whiskey lining its shelves like liquid gold. It was often a source of merriment and camaraderie (shifters flocking there like a certain yellow bear did honey pots), though Svarbjörn knew there would be none of that sort of thing that morning.

Seated in the rightmost of three barstools was another broad, scruffy man. He was wearing a dark pair of military pants and boots, topped with a lighter square-cut tank and leather jacket.

"Lobjörn…" said the Bear King dubiously, reaching the stool on the far left.

The apparent ruler of the Tensas River Basin didn't answer, his elbows planted firmly on the edge of the bar, fingers clasped and against his chin.

Svarbjörn removed his leather vest, flexed his shoulders, dropped the vest onto the middle stool between them, and sat down.

"Your *Highness*…" came a reply at last.

Lobjörn wasn't looking over to the King, rather the vest with disgust. It was black and adorned with colored patches. The words "Black Skulls MC" ran in an arch along the top rocker, while the center pie was a white bear skull with green fire in its eyes. The bottom proudly stated Morgan City.

"Or…" Lobjörn sneered bitterly, "would you rather me address you as 'Club President'?"

"Oh come now, my fellow *King*, is there really a need to be so irate?" Svarbjörn prodded; he could poke fun at titles just as easily. Eyeing one of the tawny liquor bottles, he wondered if it was too early to crack one open and down the whole thing.

"That would depend on the reason for this little meeting of yours," Lobjörn chuckled, sitting upright. He adjusted a chain around his neck before combing the fingers of both hands through his hair. "Tell me, whatever is so pressing that I had to be summoned to this rank place at such an early hour? Could we not have met any closer than *two-hundred miles* from home?"

"Two-hundred miles from *your* home, Lobjörn. This place is mine."

"Touché," Lobjörn replied, looking around as if searching for something redeeming about the surroundings. He didn't find anything. "An obvious oversight on my part. Still, I am the slightest bit offended that we couldn't meet up at Grand Lake."

"Let's hope that a meeting at Grand Lake isn't necessary," Svarbjörn stated coolly. It was the location of the Atchafalaya Throne, and a place where important matters were taken care of if they couldn't be handled elsewhere. Svarbjörn caught a fiery glare from his counterpart, adding, "Besides, this place is more personable."

"Just what you and I need," Lobjörn grumbled. He too looked toward the bar. "Well, since we are being so personable, how about a drink? Or shall I fetch one for you, Your…"

Svarbjörn stood at once, making his way around to the bottles. "If you say 'Highness', or 'Eminence', or anything of the sort again…" he warned, two glasses clinking on the wooden countertop. He poured a shot's worth in each, then tripled it. Sliding one over to Lobjörn, he raised his own glass, then downed the whole thing.

Lobjörn was not as fast, savoring the alcohol and the moment. "So, back to the reason I am here."

"That's simple enough," Svarbjörn said. His glass had already refilled. "The reason you are here is *you*." And the glass was empty again.

"Me?" Lobjörn smirked, taking another unhurried sip.

"Yes," Svarbjörn replied. "Ever since the Civil War you've been like a thorn shoved straight into my side. Why? Did I not do enough allowing you the Tensas River Basin?"

" *'Allowing'*?" Lobjörn questioned, nearly choking. "I demanded it!"

"I recall agreeing to the separation of kingdoms to preserve our numbers. We couldn't afford to devolve into a conflict like the humans were having amongst themselves. There are too few shifters in the world, not to mention the trouble we've had with the Order and all of their recent actions."

Lobjörn shifted uncomfortably in his seat, face becoming puce, voice brassy. "Oh I agree about the Order, of that there is no doubt, but let me set the record straight on the other matter. Humans. Cannot. Be. Trusted. What happened after we aided them saving their precious city? What was that dump called again; Port Hudson? What happened then? They threatened to turn on us, and they would have succeeded if the damn place wasn't lost anyway – less than a month after you exposed our kind in your vanity-driven effort to help them!"

"Is that what you think that was?" Svarbjörn bellowed. "Vanity?"

Lobjörn nodded. His look was icy. "Yes. Most definitely."

Svarbjörn could feel anger burning the alcohol in his stomach. "It was to preserve our kind."

"Preserve us how? By tradition or blending in and pretending to be the very things we are not?" Lobjörn pointed to the motorcycle vest, still innocently resting on its stool. "Like *this* for example. Taking on human guises in MC clubs and integrating into their businesses, schools, and culture. It's not preservation. It's sickening."

"It's enriching to immerse yourselves in other cultures, beliefs, and values," Svarbjörn countered. "We've been over this many times in the past, Lobjörn. My views on it haven't changed."

"Nor have mine, Svarbjörn. No, you've all just grown more human and less… superior as the years have advanced."

"Other shifter MCs like Dead Inc. up north have been successful with these efforts. As have we."

"Dead Inc.," Lobjörn scoffed. "Snake Eyes, Black Skulls, and what have you. All comically successful at losing your way. Hell, the dotards at Dead Inc. have even taken to adopting human names for themselves! Humanity is rubbing off on all the clans far too much."

Svarbjörn thought it best not to pour himself anymore to drink, else enter a situation where his fists would do a better job of communicating his thoughts. Returning the bottle to the shelf, he coughed, then asked, "Do you recall Lance Goddard?"

"The Shadow Wolf Alpha."

"Yes, one and the same. He had spent much time in this area after parting ways with his brother in the early Twentieth. He'd adopted a human name, and since you hold destruction in such high regard, he even managed to wipe out our kin in the Blue Ridge Mountains!"

"Indeed he did," Lobjörn answered. "And how did that end for the *great* Lance Goddard? In ruin, with the Order again in control of the Mountains. The Accords they'd put in place to limit our numbers did nothing good for either Ásbjörn, the Shadow Wolves, or the White Wolves that erected a façade alongside the townsfolk of

Goodman, that wretched place. Is that what you want for our people, Svarbjörn?"

"I want the best for our people, my friend. You sound just like Lance Goddard in his hatred for the future. We all need each other, especially if recent rumors about these demons are proven true."

Lobjörn withdrew, fidgeted with his hair and necklace again, then said, "I don't place my stock in the whispers of lesser mountain beasts, or humans for that matter and their frail organizations."

"King Ásbjörn a *lesser beast*? It's a good think you're drinking as slowly as you are, as I think your mind is already clouded," Svarbjörn laughed heartily. "No, he was not. That level of shortsightedness is why you will ultimately fail at whatever it is you are doing, Lobjörn."

"It was Lance's rejection of humanity that got him as far as it did, and the flimsy remnants of what he did cling to saw himself undone. Trust me, I will not make those same mistakes. We shall see who is standing at the end."

Svarbjörn raised an eyebrow. "You know, for all your talking, your voice has gotten exceedingly loud since February, Lobjörn. Do you care to explain what's prompted this change?"

"Not to you," he replied, pushing his stool away from the bar, "but I think you all will see soon enough."

"I can't help but take that statement as a threat."

"Take it as you will," Lobjörn replied, knowing that Svarbjörn wouldn't try to detain him; it wasn't in his nature. He left the remainder of his drink on the bar. "But rest assured that it is a promise."

As the Bear King of the Tensas River Basin turned to leave, his counterpart lifted the glass he left behind, and as the door closed – the sounds of the departing Triumph Bonneville rumbling into the clubhouse – he drank it.

"Well, hat certainly went better than I expected," Svarbjörn told himself before cracking his neck. There was a loud, stress-relieving *pop*. "I thought there would be at least *some* blood to clean up."

Even though Svarbjörn had thought about the blood of his brethren spilling, a great part of him never actually expected it to come to fruition. Lobjörn would prove him wrong, far sooner than the Bear King of the Atchafalaya River Basin would have ever dreamed.

Chapter 5

BILLY ARNETT HAS A RUN-IN

Wednesday April 3, 2013

1

Blood…

Billy tried his best to suppress the urge to bathe in it.

Meat…

Billy tried his best to suppress the urge to feast on it.

Cooper…

Billy tried his best to suppress the urge to –

"Ah, finally!" Cooper exclaimed as Billy came around the corner of the First Baptist church off Sullivan Street. "I was wondering when you'd get here, sleepy head!"

A week had passed since Billy had undergone the Change; since he'd viciously attacked both Cooper and Alyssa in the hospital room. Though outwardly all seemed fine, beneath that thin layer Billy was a jumbled mess of conflicting thoughts and emotions. He believed both his friends had to be too. Part of him was the same guy (a prime target for bullying like Cooper had been), but a dark and growing side wanted to give everyone that had made his life miserable trouble. The bloody, pulpy kind of trouble.

"Yeah," Billy said blushingly, "I was taking a nap and, um, forgot to set the alarm."

Billy saw Alyssa's eyes flick over toward Cooper's, their looks telling each other that they were worried about how long Billy was sleeping versus the time he was awake. He pretended like he didn't notice, though he carried the same concern himself.

What is happening to you, Billy?

The ABCs had decided to meet that evening to have some much needed fun. It was something that used to be a near daily thing, now sorely missing from their lives. Cooper had suggested a rooftop run, similar to the jaunts he'd told them about to get adjusted to his improved human athletics. But this time Cooper wouldn't be doing it alone, he would be with his friends, or rather his pack.

"Alright, follow me," Cooper said, leading them to the other side of the red-bricked building. They came to a small parking lot just outside of a daycare drop off area. Above the door was an overhang. Cooper pointed a single finger toward the roof above that. "First thing's first, I'll meet you up there."

This time it was Alyssa and Billy that looked at each other, then the roof with concern.

"Trust me," Cooper said. "It'll be a blast."

"But, what if someone sees us?" Billy asked.

"Then they'll have completed the first of several quick steps to the mental asylum," Cooper replied jokingly. "Seriously, the area's been less crowded since Saint Patrick's Day. Folks are scared and probably aren't going to venture out at night anytime soon. We should be fine."

Alyssa nodded in agreement. "Okay then, Coop. Show us how it's done."

Billy bit his lower lip and watched as Cooper ran up to the side of the building, jumped against it then – twisting – vaulted toward the overhang. He pulled himself onto the small ledge easily, took a short breath, and jumped the rest of the way to the second story roof.

"See," Cooper said to them. "Easy peasy. Okay baby, your turn."

Alyssa took a deep breath and was off, gracefully leaping and spinning like a gymnast against the wall, to the overhang, then the roof.

"Ta-da," she said, a bit out of breath. With hands on hips she looked down to Billy, still biting that lip. "Come on *William*! You can do it!"

Billy hated that name, but ignored the jab; his heart was beating heavily in his chest and it felt like he was on stage ready to sing in front of a massive crowd but had forgotten all the words.

"You've got this man!" Cooper encouraged.

"Whelp," Billy sighed, "the show must go on."

With heavy steps the stocky guy ran toward the wall, preparing himself to jump.

"Jump and twist," he chanted. "Jump and twist. Jump…" and Billy smashed into the side of the church with the force of a freight train. Falling backwards, he'd left a notable crack in the brickwork.

Alyssa and Cooper winced.

"Ouch," she hissed through gritted teeth while he knelt, peering over the edge.

"Billy, you okay?"

After a groan, Billy raised a shaky thumb. It fell back to his side a second later, and he just laid there.

"Is he getting up?" Alyssa asked after a few minutes. Crouching beside Cooper, she grabbed hold of his shoulders and rested her chin on one.

"I think so," Cooper replied as Billy stirred, then stood.

"I… I think I'm ready to try again," Billy said, rubbing the back of his head.

"Alright buddy," Cooper said confidently. "We'll see you up top."

Alyssa and Cooper stood up; Billy repositioned himself and sprinted toward the wall again.

This time he kicked off without a hitch, spinning in the air to grab hold of that pesky overhang which was giving him the most fear. Arms straining a little (his grip slipped), Billy shuffled up the edge while trying not to look down, then joined the other two on top of the church.

"There you go!" Alyssa said proudly, patting Billy in the middle of his back. "Holding up okay?"

"I… am…" He was panting, but recovered quickly. Looking around the rooftop, he saw that it went up one more level.

THREE stories off the ground?

Billy had disliked heights since he was young, but even more since climbing a bus-sized obelisk in the bowels of a crumbling

Order Vault, not to mention being clutched in the jaws of the tall Gray Mother…

"Billy?"

He shuddered; it was Cooper.

"You ready for the next part of this?"

Billy looked at the rise in the roof line again. Gulping, he wanted to say, "No way," but Alyssa seemed to encourage him without a word. Her simple smile was enough, and it reinforced in Billy the strength of the trio's friendship.

"So," Cooper said. "The plan is to jump across Sullivan Street, then carry on toward downtown and the square by means of the rooftops."

"Sounds doable," Alyssa said before surveying the path they'd be taking. She sputtered after staring at it for a minute.

"We can take it one step at a time," Cooper said to Billy, who looked about ready to take a dump in his sweat pants (or was smelling a load freshly dropped).

Billy giggled nervously. "If you say so, Coop."

"Oh, I do," Cooper said, and with a wink he dashed along the church at tremendous speed. He sprung up to the third floor in a single bound, then over Sullivan Street to a building on the other side of the road. There he waited.

Alyssa followed, Billy bringing up the rear as the two got to the third floor of the church and leaped off…

…landing across the street with Cooper.

Cooper started to open his mouth to congratulate them, but Billy didn't stop, continuing to run while he had the courage to do so.

His feet thumped, then soared, then thumped again as he raced across those previously unreachable rooftops. It was a remarkable feeling – the sensation of flying – filling him with a sense of freedom that he had not had in, well, ever. Billy looked up toward the faint stars wheeling overhead (the wind causing his eyes to tear up) then down to the streets which passed by as a gray blur.

Alyssa and Cooper were closing the gap, laughter filling the darkening sky. All three bore beaming smiles, for it was a good night with good friends. Billy took it upon himself to go first, and soon they were all howling with tremendous joy at the moon.

2

It was undeniable by the time the trio landed on the roofs above Center Street that their bond had grown.

Billy had maintained the lead, coming down first. Alyssa was next, Cooper gladly being third.

"That was amazing!" Alyssa said gleefully, sniffling to stop her nose from running.

On the other hand, Billy used his forearm to wipe his snot away, nodding profusely in agreement. "Yeah…" he wheezed. "That… was… incredible."

Cooper laughed. "Heck yes it was! I have to tell you two: it was far, *far* better with company."

"Well, with folks like us," Alyssa responded, "I'd expect nothing less."

"Shall we?" Cooper asked, pointing toward the edge of the roof. Below was a narrow alleyway he'd dropped into many times over the last few months. "Ladies first."

Alyssa stepped toward the edge and glanced down; Billy too. Although it was dark, he could still make out a lot of detail – from the tufts of smelly garbage in the corners to a small mouse scurrying between them.

These eyes would have helped during my driving test, Billy lamented, knowing full well that the lack of a car would have been the next hurdle to overcome.

Alyssa dropped to the pavement below, her landing soft and graceful. Cooper did the same, while Billy managed to land less than graciously (yet somehow, it was perfectly fitting).

Billy hobbled out of the alley, stepping onto Center Street. He moved toward a nearby bench where Cooper and Alyssa were sitting. Leaning against the back rest while they occupied the seat itself, he asked, "What's the plan?"

"I figure you're hungry," Alyssa said, and with eyes bulging quickly added, "for pizza or something like that."

Billy frowned, knowing that his appetite had been leaning toward "canine" ever since the Change. He cast a side glance toward Cooper, whose cheek had fully healed, yet Billy could see the gash in his mind's eye – fresh, red, leaking.

"That sounds good," Cooper said, grinning back at Billy, "but as much as I love Castillo's, I wish Kimmy's was open again."

"Me too," Alyssa added. "Do you think she's ever going to reopen? A hot, sticky apple fritter would be amazing right now."

"I hope she does," Billy said, "I'm missing the strawberry ring donuts the most; they reminded me of Homer Simpson."

"Haha, for a time there you were looking like ol' Homer," said Cooper cheerfully. "Hmmm, the flavor I think I savor is the Boston cream, but I'm not sure we're going to have those anymore. She was shaken up pretty badly with all the wolves attacking outside her front door."

"Not to mention *you*," Alyssa added, speaking of Cooper transforming into a monster right in front of Alyssa, Kimmy, and all her early morning patrons. "I'd think if she was open you would be the last person she'd want in the store, or anywhere within a thousand miles."

"But you know me," Cooper said. "I'm harmless."

"Yes, but they don't. At least not the version we do."

Cooper sighed; his stomach grumbled. Castillo's it was then. Standing, he helped Alyssa up and locked arms with her. "Billy," he began but quickly faded, "do you want to share a large –"

Billy was walking toward an ominous, shadowy figure. It was tall and slender.

"Billy…" Cooper called.

He didn't reply, marching forward in almost a zombie-like state.

"Billy…" Alyssa repeated.

He grew angry, especially when the figure stepped out of the shadows and into the cone of a streetlight. Billy recognized him as Ralph Bester.

Cooper clenched his fists together, more to do with Billy than Ralph. "Now's not a good time," Cooper warned.

Ralph was a junior from Goodman High School. Billy remembered him from the time he tried to bully Cooper in the school's cafeteria. It was late September, and it didn't end well for Ralph, who received a broken nose from Cooper for his troubles. Yet, as an unexpected bonus, it did spark the largest food fight in the school's history.

Delicious food… Billy thought hungrily.

What Cooper didn't know (because Billy didn't tell him) was that Ralph decided to exact some revenge in early November.

Cooper was becoming untouchable, but Billy? Oh that burly kid was just a nobody in somebody's shadow.

"Billy Arnett's so poor he can't even pay attention..." the mocking voices of Ralph and his cronies prodded.

After school one day, when Cooper and Alyssa were busy at Spring Park, Billy was walking alone along the north end of Grove Road, just thinking. That's when Ralph's gang descended on him, Ralph himself striking Billy in the back of the head with a two by four, sending him to the ground…

"Billy's so poor his mom cuts out the pockets of his jeans so he can have something to play with…" they jeered.

The punches that came next were painful, but nothing more than the kicking. Rubber soles met soft skin, causing merciless stinging that spread out from each and every one of the dozen or so blows to his chest, shoulders, and back…

Presently, Billy and Ralph were face to face, Ralph's expression one of revulsion.

"What are you even doing here?" Cooper asked.

"None of your business, Bennett," Ralph snapped. "Last I checked it's a free country, and I can walk wherever I please."

Billy let out a deep growl, drawing Ralph's attention.

"Except this poor, fat piece of shit is in my way. Move," he ordered hatefully.

"Ralph," Alyssa pleaded when she saw Billy's fingers curl. "Please, just stop."

"Shut up," he spat, "and go back to whoring yourself out like the ditzy bitch you are."

Cooper stepped forward furiously. However, before he managed to take another, Billy had pounced. "No!" he yelled.

Billy was atop Ralph, pummeling him mercilessly with his fists. His head bobbed maniacally. "Softer…" he slurred, eyes wide and malevolent.

"What the fuck?" Ralph shouted. "Get off me!"

Billy wasn't listening.

"Cooper!" Alyssa looked around hysterically. Nobody had heard Ralph yelling yet, but that didn't mean someone wouldn't come around one of the many corners soon. "We have to get Billy off him!"

Cooper was trying, but Billy was incredibly strong in that state.

"Softer… must… be… softer…"

Cooper had heard those words before; he'd even spoken them himself. They were like those of Derek Wilder so many Halloweens ago, the day Cooper had first met (and saved) Billy. Things had come full circle, and he would have to do it again.

"No!" Ralph screamed when Billy seized his arm, salivating.

"MEAT!"

Cooper snatched Billy's hand – the one holding Ralph like a vise – and using both his and all his strength, he pulled them apart. "Alyssa, go!"

She wasted no time scurrying around to Ralph's back, dragging him away from Billy. His teeth were gnashing, biting the air as if devouring a banquet.

Cooper yanked Billy in the opposite direction, pulling him away from the other two as they retreated. Then, he slipped on an uneven bit of sidewalk and overbalanced, dropping to the ground on his side. Cooper's grip loosened, and Billy was free.

He rushed toward Ralph, who kicked him in the face. Billy grabbed his ankle and started twisting, his mouth clamping down on Ralph's shoes.

There was a flash of silver.

"Sorry buddy, but I had to be prepared," Cooper whispered, having pulled out a switchblade from his back pocket. He thrust the knife into Billy's upper arm, which smoked as he roared in pain, letting go of Ralph's foot.

Alyssa tugged, managing to drag Ralph's body to an intersection with Market Street. From there, Ralph scampered away on all fours at first, screaming into the night.

Alyssa rejoined Cooper a few moments later, watching Billy. He was bowled over, left arm still smoking like a chimney stack.

"Has he calmed down any?" Alyssa asked.

Cooper shook his head, Billy turning in their direction. Tears of confusion and frustration were streaming down his face. He was lost.

Help me! Billy's mind screamed. *Meat… I HATE THIS! Soften the meat… I HATE MYSELF!*

But Cooper and Alyssa couldn't hear his thoughts, only judge his words and actions. Their friend was in horrendous turmoil, and Billy knew they were just as lost as he on what to do.

"Everything is going to be alright, Billy," Alyssa said softly. "We'll work through this."

He snorted, eyes burning and red, longing for the life before his cursed one turned worse.

"This isn't you, man," Cooper said reassuringly, taking a seat right next to Billy on the sidewalk. He put an arm around him. "This is the Gray Mother's doing; not yours man. Not yours one damn bit."

"How can you be so sure?" Billy asked. His voice broke.

"Because we know you," Alyssa said. "The real you, not this… *thing*… that is trying to take over."

"The real Billy Arnett wouldn't let anything beat him," Cooper added. "Especially anything evil. I mean you stood up to some pretty mean stuff before."

"Yeah, the Gray Mother was no joke," said Alyssa. "Besides, you have the two of us to help you. Remember that; we aren't here to hurt…"

"…or hinder you," Cooper finished, his hand on Billy's raised knee sealing the deal.

Billy exhaled, extending his legs. He put his hands on the pavement, which was warm, and looked skyward. "I appreciate it guys. I'm still worried though."

"Wouldn't expect you not to be," Cooper said. "So, are you still up for that food, or was Ralph's shoe enough for you tonight?"

Alyssa tried hard not to laugh, only doing so when Billy did first.

"You two go ahead," he said solemnly. "I… I just need to think right now."

Billy could tell that Cooper didn't want to leave him, especially in that state (and right after he'd attacked Ralph in the open). Alyssa looked the same, but more understanding.

"Coop," she said, "let's give him some space and time. It's going to be a busy day tomorrow anyway, remember? The whole reason for tonight's fun."

Cooper's expression became weighty. Something pushed all other thoughts in his mind away.

"You nervous?" Billy asked, his turn to be comforting.

Cooper nodded.

"It's going to be okay," Billy whispered. "*We're* going to be okay."

Billy would always be glad to have friends like Cooper and Alyssa around (and hoped they knew it; he didn't say it often enough), especially since they took care of him when he had run-ins like that night. Cooper would need that kind of support the next day, when they would venture up into the mountains for a ceremony they only knew as The Climb.

Billy suspected that Cooper knew more but had been keeping those details close to his chest. He wondered if it was so they didn't worry, since he was likely doing enough for all three of them.

Chapter 6

SADNESS AND SURVIVAL

1

Billy was walking home along Center Street, having said goodbye to Cooper and Alyssa outside the Italian restaurant. As he moved north, hands buried deep in his second hand pants pockets (there were indeed holes in them), he found himself mulling over the past and thinking about the future – especially since everything he was planning to do had since shifted, pun most certainly intended.

It was like the world had opened up since finding out the monsters he enjoyed watching on TV shows and movies were real.

Hopefully not all of them are, Billy thought, spine tingling over some of the nastier creations he'd seen over the years.

Yet, the world also seemed more closed off. There were fewer people to share achievements, goals, and life in general with – especially with his mom and dad… gone.

As the values of passing houses dropped much faster than the temperature, and the spaces between them grew larger and more filled with junk, Billy found that he felt less anxious and depressed about living on the poorer north side of Goodman, but more worried about where he would be going now that the opportunity to do so was laid before him.

He didn't want to work at his father's business anymore (Rabun Paving, not a stone's throw from their front porch), nor attend college in Goodman – if at all. The memories, all of them, were too sinking.

He knew that Cooper was in a similar boat, even though his father was a royal jackass. Their house had been paid off due to Roland's "unfortunate" death, though now that he owned it, Cooper didn't want it (if he ever did at all.) As he thought more about it, Billy recalled an Order representative stating point blank that they were doing that as a nicety. Since he was an adult he could have been left to fend for himself, but since they'd assisted, and he had been turned into a shifter anyway, Cooper would have to register with them under the Accords.

They haven't seen me about that registration yet, Billy thought. *Hmmm.*

He wondered how long it would take for someone in the Order Headquarters to read Dr. Ross' official report on the "unofficial" gas leak at Goodman Hospital, which just so happened to occur during the night of the first full moon after a massive werewolf attack in the town.

Probably not long at all... Billy surmised, half expecting a representative to be waiting for him when he got home.

He hoped that there would be enough time for the life insurance money to arrive from the plan his dad had set up through work. Enough time just in case he had to leave.

Hopefully it doesn't come to that, he thought, but Billy knew that hope was only half the battle.

Billy continued on Center Street for a little while longer, stopping into Schneck's grocery for some potato chips (salt and vinegar) which he opened and ate the rest of the way along Cherry Lane.

A few minutes later, the familiar and dispiriting sight of that old, gray single-wide trailer loomed ahead. There was no Order representative waiting to sign his rights away, yet even though it was a clear night, Billy could feel a fog around the place.

Stepping on the groaning wood steps, he walked onto the dilapidated deck, its flaking maroon paint doing nothing to stop images of blood and gore flooding his mind. Shaking it off – or trying to at least – Billy briskly walked past the run down couches he and Cooper would sit on after school, and just before he reached the door (his arm already outstretched), he heard his dad's voice.

"That is the second of two rings my own father had given to me years ago; a few after Billy was born. The first one was white and symbolized purity and hope… This one is jet black, symbolizing life's challenges and struggles to overcome."

Billy paused. Grabbed his chain.

"We've seen the bruises, and heard the excuses Cooper, and trust me when I say: we know… Since Billy considers you a brother and because you're more than welcome here at our place as one of our own… I would like you to have it."

Billy shut his eyes briefly, then let go of the chain and continued inside. It was difficult that night, more than it had been before.

The front door squeaked closed slowly, the living room greeting him with darkness. The bulbs that had been in both end table lamps (seemingly since the day he was born) had blown at the same time. Luckily, Billy could see well enough to make his way across the beige carpet to the kitchen.

That central, heartwarming place used to be alive. That night, and each one ever since it lost two thirds of its soul, it was cold, unwelcoming, and lifeless. Billy attempted to breeze through, but paused by the fridge. He stared at the dining table, eyes wide as saucers.

He saw his dad, a pale memory, sitting in his chair. Toiling away with paperwork, his mother swooped in a short time later, giving her husband a gentle kiss on the forehead. In her hand on one of their gleaming white plates was a decadent slice of chocolate cake. Scrumptious, she walked to the other side of the table and handed it off to…

Nobody.

Billy snapped out of it. There was nobody there in that trailer. No smells of roast beef, mashed potatoes, chocolate cake, or pecan pie. He was alone, Brenda and Branson Arnett – Mom and Dad – gone forever.

Billy tried his best to compose himself, but couldn't bear anymore.

Walking away, he headed to the back of the trailer (a "Danger Zone" sign still on his door – appropriate now more than ever). Entering the untidy space that was his bedroom, he crashed on the bed, but instead of falling asleep again, he wept.

2

The same Wednesday that Billy Arnett cried himself to sleep, others nearly eight-hundred miles southwest could not sleep if they tried.

Svarbjörn walked up the gentle slope of a hill, its mossy ground springy, while the air above held a similar spongy quality. Normally pleasant, the dark woods were ominous, the trees themselves looking like malevolent tree spirits of old. They seemed to close in around him – a trick of a stressed mind – but the Bear King quickened his pace nonetheless. He made way toward a pair of orange lamps about a hundred feet away, their glow the only trace of light around him. It was his path to follow out of the gloom.

When closer, the lamps revealed themselves as giant snails, their auburn glow falling out from cores of luminous white. Moving slowly around the tree trunks they clung to, amber streaks of jelly were in their wake and scented like cloves.

Svarbjörn paused, the way ahead blocked by forest litter and prickly vines. He adjusted the collar of his heavy fur robe, beneath which he wore a sort of leather monstrosity that did not do a man his size any favors in making walking an easy task.

Why the hell does a bear shifter have to wear this thing? he wondered, tradition overriding his wants that evening.

Taking a deep and pleasant breath, he pricked one of his fingers on his woody crown, then touched it to the closest thorn, the vines pulling away at once. They retreated into the nourishing ground, leaving an archway behind for him to pass under. Once he did it was like the foreboding feeling remained at the passage. An overwhelming sense of ease and calm wafted through the crisp air.

Svarbjörn had entered the Glade of the Atchafalaya Throne. The clearing at Grand Lake was vast and circular, each side sweeping with massive trees that rose tall like columns, then spread a curtain of blue flowers and green leaves to cover the area like a dome.

Svarbjörn saw that was not alone.

Within the space were two other men. The one on the left was the more uptight of the two, wearing formal robes in earthen tones that flowed over the lines of his body. The right one was shorter, more muscular, and far more roguish in appearance. Dressed in a simple denim vest and trousers with no shirt beneath, he was adorned with several wolf and tribal tattoos, along with a small bull ring in the center of his nose.

"Ah! Welcome my friends," Svarbjörn said, approaching with his huge arms outstretched. He hugged each in turn, addressing the robed man as Warryn, and the other as Rikolf. "Yes, yes, welcome."

"Thank you, Your Eminence," said Warryn.

Rikolf stared at the Bear King awkwardly. "I'm so glad we don't wear that sort of thing, ever," he said, Warryn casting a wicked look his way.

Svarbjörn did not get angry, instead bellowing with deep laughter that Rikolf joined him in. "I *wish* I didn't have to!"

Warryn, ever the serious one, cut through the cheerfulness with concern. "Indeed I wish we were all meeting under different circumstances that allowed for merriment," he said, brown eyes squinting as he looked to each of the other shifters in turn.

"Agreed," Svarbjörn answered darkly, making way for the throne. "I think we are running out of options and time."

The large structure was hewn out of a tree, still living, rimmed with ornate carvings and dappled with luminous flowers of many colors. Svarbjörn sat in it, a loud *thud* a result, and the other two repositioned themselves to each side.

"So are there any updates?" Rikolf asked, unsure he wanted to know the answer given the level of Warryn's solemnity. "The last I heard he was still threatening communities in Franklin Parish."

"I wish that were all," Warryn said gravely.

Rikolf could not hide his look of surprise.

"Lobjörn has recently been thumping his chest as far as Rapides Parish," Svarbjörn relayed.

"What?"

"Yes." Svarbjörn confirmed that Rikolf was indeed not hearing things incorrectly. "The outskirts of Alexandria to be precise, which is why Everard isn't here. Additionally…"

"There is more?"

Svarbjörn looked grave. "Yes… as of tonight… he's also advanced toward Lafayette."

Rikolf was stunned into silence. *How is this possible?* his expression asked on his word's behalf.

"I do not think Lobjörn knows that we know about his latest movements," Warryn reported, his golden eyes so wide against his mocha skin they appeared to blaze. "This move to Lafayette is a bold one indeed."

"Yeah, that's within fifty miles of my pack at Vermilion Bay!" Rikolf said anxiously. "So he has not done anything yet, other than ruffle feathers?" He looked to Warryn. "No pun or offense intended."

Warryn actually cracked a smile. "None taken, and to answer your question: no. He has not made any brash moves that would indicate anything beyond simple movements, but that could change at any time. My avian scouts were first to pick this up during your travels here."

"Then it's a good thing I went northeast, otherwise…"

"I am sure you'd have stumbled upon him yourself, and not have been so lucky in your escape on the ground – even if transformed."

"So," Svarbjörn grumbled, interrupting their conversation. "To the matter at hand. Are we to call a Gathering?"

"Damn right we are," Rikolf said sternly.

"I think it is a necessity," Warryn seconded.

"Then it's settled," Svarbjörn confirmed. "We shall convene as quickly as we can without leading on about our knowledge. Monday perhaps? We need to hear from the neighboring clans to see how to deal with this problem."

"Agreed," said Warryn.

"What on Earth is his motive?" Rikolf asked. "His goal?"

"I don't believe there is one," Svarbjörn replied. "Frankly, it's like he's possessed."

"Hmmm," Warryn mumbled. "Indeed, it is like something has managed to unlock monstrous secrets and allowed them to spill across the lands. It is not a coincidence that all these dark rumors and Lobjörn's actions all arrived at the same time."

Svarbjörn grumbled in approval.

"Regardless," Rikolf cut in, scarlet eyes raging, "I am not going to go down without a fight."

Chapter 7

THE CLIMB

Thursday April 4, 2013

1

The morning came far too quickly for Cooper's liking, and as the sun assaulted his eyesight from dawn to its current position near one o'clock, he regretted eating that extra calzone at Castillo's the night before.

"You really don't want to eat that do you?" Alyssa's cautionary question (that was really a statement) resounded in his mind while he trudged step by slow step up the shrub-studded mountainside.

The trio were in the expansive Jameson Preserve to the east of Goodman, reaching the decimated bear kingdom (that their former ally Ásbjörn called home) about an hour earlier. Crossing the Chattooga River which bordered that territory, they ventured beyond.

Cooper paused to rest, shading his eyes as he looked out to the horizon toward North Carolina. "I can definitely see why they're called the Blue Ridge Mountains now," he stated, the grand view of an unbroken chain of ridges wrapped in a soft, blue hue was hauntingly beautiful (and one that he'd never seen from the lower perspective the town afforded).

"And... I can definitely see... why this ceremony... is called 'The Climb'," Billy added, cardio still not his friend despite the changes.

Cooper turned, now staring across the frayed backpack strap slung over his shoulder. He spotted Alyssa nearby in a cute hiking outfit and boots; she was munching on a piece of beef jerky. Billy was lagging behind about twenty feet, looking like he should have eaten that extra calzone Cooper had for the energy.

"How much longer, anyway?" Billy asked. "My legs are killing me!"

"An hour more, maybe?"

Billy groaned.

"You know, you could shift into beast form to make things a little easier on yourself," Cooper told him. "You too, baby."

"Only if you do, man," Billy replied, hoping Cooper would follow up with an unequivocal "yes."

"You know that I can't," Cooper said regrettably, wishing he could, "Ceremony rules and all."

"Yeah, yeah, *rules*," Billy nattered, his eyes sinking to the rocks before looking further east. "For some strange reason the new wolf Alpha has to arrive in non-wolf form to this party."

"Think of it as symbolic," Cooper laughed.

"Crazy more like."

"Symbolic or crazy, we're in this with you the whole way," Alyssa added, walking over to Billy. She handed off the rest of her beef jerky. He took it as she looked back toward the Chattooga. "So, Ásbjörn is just gone? I can't believe he'd just abandon his home after being there for all that time."

Billy shoved food in his mouth, and while chewing noisily said, "In a way I can see why. Lance had everyone killed; Ásbjörn's friends, his mate, everyone he held dear. The place probably reminded him a lot of them, and their absence."

Cooper saw Alyssa frown. Her parents were still alive, so she couldn't know the pain Billy carried. He was glad she didn't.

Even I can't fully understand what you're going through buddy; my Pop was a real winner, Cooper mulled. *Add all this Gray Mother crap on top of that and well, hell, I would have thrown myself down a very deep, moonless well by now.*

"Any idea where he went?" Alyssa asked, returning to her middle hiking position.

Billy shrugged, as did Cooper.

"All I know from Dr. Ross," Cooper said, "is that he saw both Ásbjörn and the other Journeyman that helped us when he was in New York for his debrief."

"That big guy with the sledgehammer?" Billy asked.

Cooper nodded, resuming the hike. "He went on to Europe; Ireland I think. As for Ásbjörn, he never came back here, heading out for parts unknown."

"How sad," Alyssa said, slowly walking forward.

Billy was less than enthusiastic about hiking anymore. He shuffled his feet, picking up pace only when Cooper called back to tell him to hurry up.

2

The ABCs continued to march along the spectacular mountain ridge, about twenty miles outside of Goodman. They passed weathered hemlock, spotting bobcats in the distance. Billy was sure he saw a lone wolf too.

"I wonder who that was," Billy said innocently.

Cooper chuckled, until he realized Billy was being serious. "I'm not sure," he said, "but something tells me that not *all* wildlife is supernatural, buddy."

"Bummer," Billy replied.

"On that note," Alyssa added inquisitively, looking to Cooper, "what *are* the differences in shifters?"

"Like, the kinds?"

Alyssa nodded.

"Grayson didn't tell me too much about the different species."

Cooper was referring to Grayson Manning, a stock market trader and real estate investor that had made a name for himself in town (not to mention a lot of money). He lived on a large estate downtown, and was the father of the school's star quarterback Liam Manning – former bully to Cooper, now deceased by Lance Goddard's hand. As if that weren't enough to fill Cooper's life with unending joy, Grayson was also Alpha of the White Wolf Pack that resided in Goodman, and the brother of Lance Goddard himself.

"Surely Grayson told you something," Alyssa pressed.

"Well, I know there are wolves…"

"Duh," said Billy. "Obviously."

"And…" Cooper continued, eyes squinting in that *just say something else, smartass* manner, "bears. He also mentioned boars, and something called 'aves'?"

Alyssa watched a flock of swallows taking flight as the trio passed by an oak tree. "Birds," she said reverently. "Aves are birds."

"How's that work then?" Billy asked. "Shrinking down to the size of a pigeon? That's not something I'd be boasting about."

Alyssa gave another laugh, then clasped her hands over her mouth in case any of the lingering swallows were listening.

Billy smiled. "See, you know exactly what I mean. I'd much rather turn into a huge beast than a chicken."

"Cooper," Alyssa started, Billy's statement the engine of her train of thought. "Did Grayson make any mention of what Billy… actually is?"

"He did tell me some stuff about the origins of wolves. Sounded rather complicated to me, so I may have misunderstood some of it …"

"Not just werewolves then?" Billy asked, listening intently.

Cooper shook his head. "I wish. Seems no matter how you cut it the Gray Mother is… or was… the origin of them all."

Alyssa listened too as they walked. "No telling how old she was…"

"She gave birth directly to purebred Primal werewolves."

"Those things that came popping out of Her in the Vault?" Billy asked, recalling those terrifying, upright grotesqueries with twisted arms and sharp teeth.

"Yep. Grayson said some call them the epitome of werewolf kind, but they only had just enough intelligence to be dangerous. If you got bitten by one and didn't get eaten alive, you'd become a werewolf that could walk upright like they did and only change during the full moon. If you didn't get enough food after the Change, then you'd degrade, or upgrade in some people's views, to a Primal."

"Boom! B monster movies!" Billy exclaimed. "Knew that came from somewhere."

"Now, the Gray Mother would also give birth to different kinds of natural mutations, which is where Grayson nearly lost me. Some of those mutations were directly werewolves – as in no Primal bite was needed. Those weren't locked by the full moon and could change at whim after the first one."

"Like us then?" Alyssa asked.

"Close, but no..." Cooper replied, and Alyssa looked puzzled. "We're the *other* kind of mutation – a wolf shifter. They're almost the same as a werewolf with the distinction of having a more traditional but still large wolf form. Grayson said you can recognize them by their eyes – which look human but are blue, yellow, orange, or even black in some cases."

"Lost yet?" Billy asked Alyssa. "Because I am."

"Haha," Cooper chuckled. "Seems wolf shifters are capable of talking too, if that helps distinguish them in your mind."

"So like Akela from *The Jungle Book*," Billy remarked. "Check."

"That sounds better than a Primal for sure as the 'perfect form'," Alyssa added.

"Right," said Cooper.

"But, neither Billy or us fit in that mold," she pointed out.

"Correct," Cooper replied. "Grayson indicated there were two other forms – rare but powerful."

Billy readied himself.

"First, in very rare cases, a lone wolf or subordinate shifter can harness the power of an Alpha if they have a worthy heart. The eyes become green in that case, and the person can assume a Primal-like shape if needed while maintaining full consciousness and speech."

"That sounds really familiar," Billy noted, "and me?"

"Grayson didn't know too much, but he referred to the potential for you being something called a dire wolf shifter. Apparently it's the rarest form of all since it can only happen after a *bite* from the Gray Mother herself."

"Yeah, I'm not sure many make it past that point alive. She definitely wanted more than just my leg for dinner," Billy joked, shaking his right leg as if it were asleep. "He tell you any more details?"

"No, mainly because he didn't know. Seems the only other details he knew and we can confirm is that your hunger is more severe and your beast is huge."

"Well… alrighty then," Billy said smugly with an eyebrow waggle, wiping away some sweat. He started rubbing his sore thighs. "So this Climb thingy is a way to get you, as a lone Alpha to take over a pack?"

Cooper sighed. It was full of worry. "Sort of. More that I'm an outsider than a loner. The Climb is apparently the ceremony for me to take over as Shadow Alpha. It happens when wolves that have a stake aren't a direct descendent of the former Alpha by birth, Lance in this case."

"Right. Lance is *gone*," Alyssa said pointedly, "and you got rid of him. I don't see why there's a need for all this. You should be able to have that title."

"I wish, but things aren't ever that simple. It's tradition mainly, but *technically* the Gray Mother is the one that got rid of Lance, and Billy is the one that got rid of her. But since he's not a Shadow Wolf at all…"

"…I have no stake or claim on the pack," Billy gulped (part of him had to suppress the hunger since having a 'stake' reminded him of eating a 'steak'… *meat*). "But if there's a ceremony, doesn't that imply someone can challenge you? Like, even at a wedding they throw down that bouquet like a gauntlet and challenge anyone to bring it."

"That's not quite how it works. Besides that's just in the movies, Billy," Alyssa said, chastising.

"And up until last month so were werewolves, my dear!" Billy replied obnoxiously.

"The answer's yes," Cooper interjected. "Someone can, and likely will issue a challenge. That's why I'm nervous; I don't know what to expect."

"The unexpected, as always," Billy stated matter-of-factly, and he was, of course, right.

Suddenly Cooper stopped, the hour of hiking he'd promised ended up being correct. Ahead, at the top of the climb beyond strangely unseasonal snow flurries was their destination. Alyssa grabbed Cooper's hand, Billy stepping to the other side in line with his shoulder.

"You know, now that we're here, I want to be back in town," Cooper said, chilled. Then, after taking in a deep breath, he went against his own wishes and took a step forward. "Come on then, destiny awaits."

3

Cooper led Billy and Alyssa higher, approaching the thick, green edge of a forest sprinkled with snow. Two black wolves emerged, stopping ahead of the vegetation. They stared intently with yellow eyes.

"Think those are shifters?" Billy whispered; Cooper didn't reply.

"Who are you to come here?" the rightmost wolf snarled, stepping forward with raised hackles.

The trio stopped, Cooper slightly ahead with his arms protectively to the side.

"My name is Cooper Bennett, Alpha of the –"

"We know who you are, Shadow Alpha to Be," the left wolf growled. "The she-wolf too."

"Who we do not know is that one," snarled the right wolf again, sniffing the air. "I ask again: who are you to come here?"

"That's Billy," Cooper answered. "Billy Arnett. He is with me."

The wolves growled, heads shaking.

"No, he cannot be here." The left wolf smelled the air as well. "He *must not* be here. He is a corruption, and it is –"

"It is fine by me," Cooper said firmly. "He is my friend and guest, and will be treated with respect." Cooper lowered his arms, claws emerging. "Or you will be shown none either."

Billy and Alyssa remained quiet as the two black wolves stirred in obvious conflict.

"Very well," the right wolf howled after a few minutes, "though you carry the full responsibility of this action, Alpha to Be."

Cooper relaxed, then grabbed the straps of his backpack. "I never said that I wouldn't."

With that, the two wolves turned and entered the forest, Cooper and company following close, but not too close, behind. The woods were bright and sunny despite the denseness of the trees and the weather, though there was a pervading feeling that the three of them were being watched from afar – every step, every blink, every breath.

A short time later, the wolves they were following led them into a large clearing with short grass and nuggets of rock. Overhead the sky was clear and blue, and around the edge of the woods were more black wolves, perhaps a hundred. The two wolves split, waiting on Cooper to pass. Once he did, they closed in again, stopping Alyssa and Billy in their tracks.

"Hey!" Cooper shouted. "What's the meaning of this? You said they were okay to be here!"

The right wolf spoke. "We said that we knew who the she-wolf was, and that this one could not enter. We made an exception for you in this case, but they must remain here for the rest of the Climb."

Cooper took a step forward in anger and aegis.

"Do not test our patience, Cooper Bennett. Until you are the Shadow Alpha in full, do not."

"Coop," Alyssa urged, "go on. We'll be alright."

Cooper bowed, then observed Billy. He looked so out of place and unwelcome.

Please don't freak out on me now, buddy, Cooper thought as he turned away. "Very well," he said. "Where do I go from here?"

"To the center," the left wolf advised, then the two lead Cooper's friends away.

Cooper did as instructed, feelings jumping from irritation to unease to concern. All things considered, his heart was serene in comparison, as was his breathing. Reaching the center, he stopped. All eyes – hundreds of penetrating yellow ones – were looking at him, waiting for him, counting on him to speak.

"Good afternoon," Cooper said to the gathered masses of wolves apprehensively. "My name is Cooper Bennett and I… I am here to assume the role of Shadow Alpha in place of Lance Goddard."

There came a cacophony of noise from all sides, a mix of hateful barks and growls from wolves still allied with Lance, alongside howls of agreement from those who understood the Alpha power within Cooper (far more than he did himself).

Cooper didn't know where to focus with all the racket, instead looking toward the ground. He spotted a single clover growing amidst the short grass and weeds, and a grin rose out of the anxiety to fill his face.

"I can tell by that response that there are some that do not want me here," Cooper continued. "Trust me when I say that thought has crossed my mind several times on my way here – right up to the point of passing into this very clearing. I'd challenge anyone who thinks they are so great and unafraid to say otherwise and *not* be lying.

"Taking ownership of issues is the first step to correcting the problems created by them, and there have been a lot of problems created recently, haven't there? A lot of pain and suffering. Goodman has gone to Hell and back; I've seen it first hand, as I'm sure you all have gone there too. Lance became driven by a single, selfish goal, neglecting to realize that a pack is one entity, built by the sum of its parts."

The incensed barks were overtaken by approving howls.

"Lance had the right ideas about being free, free from the Order and their Accords but also free from the chains of hatred. His hatred of humanity was misguided, you see. Now, I know what you're thinking: 'This boy has been more human than wolf,' and you know what? Yes! Yes I have. But it's about that ownership, isn't it? I did not ask to be bitten the night I was. I did not ask for this Alpha power to suddenly form inside and explode my life into ten thousand different opportunities and hurdles. But what I do ask for is the chance to use that destined authority to help us become greater than the sum of all our parts, by embracing all aspects of it: Purebred, Turned, and human alike."

Cooper looked around and saw many agreeing faces (insofar as he could make out the differences in wolf expressions). However, as he knew to expect, there was a dissenting voice amongst the throng.

"Doesn't he speak eloquently?" came a harsh, ratty voice. A mangy wolf emerged. "For a former human at least."

"Who are you?" Cooper asked.

"Rodric is my name," the wolf replied, dripping with ego. "Son of Goddard."

There were no surprised gasps from the other wolves; Cooper took it as a good sign.

"And which son might that be? Because, from my understanding, that's why I'm up here in the first place." Cooper was pointed. "Lance violated a slew of covenants by taking on way too many mates over the years, thinning his lineage to the consistency of water."

"His blood still runs thicker than the piss that flows through some *outsider's* veins."

At that point the gasps arrived, but Cooper wasn't too bothered by the insult, thinking Rodric would turn around and leave. Of course he didn't.

"Tell me Bennett, since you're the Alpha to Be, do you know of anything relative to pack hierarchy or the intricacies of our species?"

What does that have to do with anything? Cooper wondered, realizing Rodric was trying to discredit him. He replied, "Alphas, Betas, Omegas – oh my?"

"Ah, that's very funny, couching all your ignorance in empty humor."

"I see nothing empty about it," Cooper replied.

"I see *everything* empty about you," said Rodric.

"What is your point with all this?"

"The point is to highlight the fact that as a human, you do not understand the intricate nature of shifter life."

"Are you saying one can't learn?"

"Why bother to wait for your leader to learn if there is someone who already knows?"

"And I gather that someone is you?" Cooper asked, cringing.

"Yes. Me."

"Well, I don't plan on stepping down," Cooper countered.

"I didn't expect you to," Rodric replied and without another word, he lunged.

The wolf crashed into Cooper like a dark bullet, Cooper getting in a few good punches on Rodric's jaw then side.

As they battled, Cooper thought it was like fighting a less-skilled version of Liam back in school. They tussled, Rodric clamping down on Cooper's forearm.

Cooper knocked him away, then gained the upper hand (if he'd ever lost it), grabbing Rodric by the neck. The urge to shift into beast form and crush his windpipe was overwhelming, but in the end Cooper let go to melodious howls.

"Cooper Bennett is the victor!" stated one of the guardian wolves.

"Hail to the new Alpha!" said the other.

Rodric growled, readying himself to pounce again. Subordinates surrounded Cooper to protect him, teeth bared.

"Go," Cooper said to Rodric, disappointed. "You've lost."

"I do not plan on going any…"

"Go!" Cooper repeated, this time shouting. "You and any of your followers are hereby banished from the Shadow Wolves."

The surrounding wolves howled again.

"You cannot do this!" Rodric exclaimed. "I am descended from Goddard himself!"

"I can… and I did. At least honor the traditions you claim to hold dear. Otherwise, you're just as empty as you claimed my humor to be."

Rodric seemed to diminish in size, turning away.

"You're more than welcome to set up a pack of your own," Cooper added.

"As should this… *thing* there," Rodric said, tipping his head toward Billy, who was approaching with Alyssa as the light snow started to stop.

The surrounding pack wolves did not howl in agreement with Rodric, but they were not offended by the statement either.

Cooper realized that Billy's presence was going to be a problem – not with him or Alyssa, but long term with the pack's order. His gut sank like a stone just thinking about the decision he would have to make.

Yet, that could wait for another day. "Not sure that was the right thing to do," Cooper told Billy, whispering it as they got close.

"That's the trouble with choices," Billy replied. "You never know if you've really made the right one until later on; often when it's too late."

Chapter 8

THE CITY BENEATH THE SEA

Monday April 8, 2013

1

The golden lights of the Crescent City twinkled beneath a cloudy, twilight sky like the matching moon above. The streets were packed with people whose ears were filled with music and bellies filled with an endless supply of cocktails and cuisine. However, the busiest regional port since the 1700s had not always been so amiable.

The area had exchanged hands through a history of wars from the French, to British, to Spanish, culminating with the Great New

Orleans Fire in 1788 (and again just six years later in 1794), a sad spectacle that engulfed most of the city and countless lives, while leaving the rest with nothing in hand but bewilderment, distress, and loss. Once rebuilt with stone and iron instead of wood, the city was again signed and traded away from Spain, back to France, who then sold its lands to the United States in 1803.

It was during the Nineteenth Century that war again came to the area, both on the surface and below. According to the Order, during the human's War of 1812, which ended up spanning three years after the British sent forces to capture New Orleans, vampires from the Germain Coven took up in the Vieux Carré, spreading their inhuman bloodlust to every shadowed corner of the city.

Approximately fifty years passed with the vampires at odds with wolf shifters in the five parishes of Jefferson, Orleans, Plaquemines, St. Bernard, and St. Tammany. The vampires drove the werewolves west toward Vermilion Bay, while they avoided the Atchafalaya region due to its unpredictable bear inhabitants.

The vampires had nearly succeeded in eliminating their wolf shifter enemy, saved only when another war between humans broke out. The American Civil War spread an ultimately involved four different shifter species – birds, bears, boars, and wolves – and it was during that period of strife that the shifters undid the Germain Coven and their hold of New Orleans. In the aftermath (seeing the toll that a civil war had on the human population and their own), the clans took it upon themselves to create an agreement known as the

Treaty of Marksville. It established boundaries not unlike the state's parishes, keeping both order and civility in the forefront for over two hundred years.

That is, until 2013, when the Bear King Svarbjörn, Aves Leader Warryn, and Vermilion Bay Alpha Rikolf agreed to call together The Gathering of old clans throughout the region. They met on April 8, in the City Beneath the Sea, to discuss their futures and the threat posed by the crazed Bear King Lobjörn.

2

Delegates from the four beast clans arrived after dark at a majestic hotel between Bourbon Street and Royal. Svarbjörn walked through the elegant interior of damask wallpaper, large oil paintings, and flowing draperies, feeling the rich history up-lit with brilliant wall sconces and illuminated by sparkling chandeliers.

He passed two hooded protectors posted at the entrance to a courtyard, nodded, and continued into an open-aired expanse surrounded by brown brick and many ferns. Scattered around were ornate tables and chairs of wrought iron, a small fountain on the far wall filling the space with the natural sound of falling water. Strands of little lights were strung from wall to wall in rows, completing the look of a forest under starlight captured in the middle of the hotel.

With him in the courtyard were fellow bear shifters, along with a trio of men that looked like they'd stepped out from *The Real*

McCoys. Outfitted in overalls, light button ups, and a mix of baseball caps and cowboy hats, the largest was Everard, Leader of the Red River Soundry (which was boar territory).

The Aves were there too. Warryn from Jean Lafitte was garbed similarly to their prior meeting, but with more sumptuous robes of gilded gray. To his sides were two females with sweeping, feathered earrings that framed their faces in gold. Leaders from Peveto Woods and Grand Isle, Svarbjörn found each to be as beautiful as the day was long.

Finally, he laid eyes on Rikolf, standing near the wall finishing a bottle of beer. Dressed more appropriately in a dark suit (but still with a nose ring), the ruddy shades of his beard were accentuated. He was flanked by two of his closest brothers: Badric his Beta – who had an air of conceit about him, and an Omega named Elric – similar in stature to the Beta, far less snooty but far more foolhardy.

Svarbjörn made his rounds, and after many greetings and short discussions, the crowd convened at their respective tables. Food and wine were present, but many (except the wolves) didn't partake, the urge to speak overriding any hunger or thirst that evening.

A lot was said of things happening within their individual lands, a few of the wider world beyond Louisiana (like the Blue Ridge Mountains to the northeast and other states to the west), but most of the discussion fell to Alexandria and Vermilion Bay where the Bear King of the Tensas River Basin was inciting unease and dread.

"Bah!" Everard bellowed, hearing enough hemming and hawing from the birds on what to do gently and civilly. "We should just storm the Tensas Basin and be done with it!"

"No, that is not our way," Svarbjörn stated, and as much as he wanted to say the complete opposite, he couldn't.

"Then what would you have us do?" Everard replied starkly. "Sit and wait until Lobjörn comes right up to bite us on our own asses?"

"You know very well that's not my intent."

"Gentlemen please," Warryn said calmly, "Lobjörn is making advances, whatever his ends and means are, with a single mind. We cannot let all of ours get in the way of figuring out how to counter him."

"Indeed," Elric spoke up, surprising everyone. "I mean, I'm even hearing talk that the forest spirits are noticing things happening."

A majority of the gathering made awkward coughing sounds, trying their best to avoid outright groans.

"That may be, Elric," said Rikolf, "but unless those forest spirits or whatever appear in this room tonight while we are all here, we cannot rely on those fairytales to help."

"But… there's been a rise in the number of gators! I've seen that with my own eyes. I have!" Elric replied. "Surely that's a sign."

Badric scoffed. "A sign that you've gone barking mad. Gators in the swamps? Oh, that's *super* out of the ordinary. Elric, those are just a bunch of old stories meant to scare old people. Forest spirits are the stuff of fantasy. Reality is needed here."

"Yeah," Elric said, shuddering as if a chill trickled down his spine. "As if demons aren't scary enough, and real?"

Badric glanced over to Elric, then slid his view toward Rikolf. "Yes, very scary and very real indeed."

Rikolf paid Badric no mind, turning his attention to Svarbjörn again. "Now *that* is something more tangible we can talk about: the Order and these supposed demons. Why are their Journeymen not helping with the Lobjörn situation?"

Svarbjörn looked to Warryn to relay the news.

"They have informed us that in keeping with the Accords, that this is a purely shifter matter, and must be dealt with internally."

"After dealing with the issues up in Goodman?" Rikolf exclaimed.

"Indeed," Warryn said. "I think the issues there highlighted the fact that they were massively unprepared since the Incursion back in 2010. Their numbers are still recovering, as are ours…"

"As for the demons?" Everard asked.

"They're a far greater threat to the Order," Svarbjörn said before Warryn had the chance, "so they're focused on dealing with them more than us squabbling animals. This is a dark threat encircling us all, and this conflict with Lobjörn is a mere distraction."

"Well, Your Eminence," said Warryn, "I wouldn't put it quite like that."

"Yet I would," said Svarbjörn. "Now, the rumors state the Noctis are spreading south, championed by one I have heard called Dajjal. Does anyone know this name?"

None did; all expressions bare.

"We must find out more. So then, we have to deal with Lobjörn quickly, before he…"

There was a loud *thud* by the courtyard's entrance, followed by another. Turning, the assembled shifters saw the protectors on the ground, unconscious (so they hoped).

"Before I what exactly?" Lobjörn asked as he strode into the area, arms overhead and touching random twinkling lights despite their heat. "Well… well… what do we have here?" he said with feigned shock. "A Gathering, without yours truly invited to the party? I have a feeling the topic of discussion might just be… me."

"What are you doing here?" Rikolf demanded, standing at his table quickly.

"Settle down, mutt."

Rikolf bit his lip; Badric tried to calm him down.

"I hear you all talking about demons and such," Lobjörn continued. "You know, there are ways to combat these threats. Threats the Atchafalaya King apparently can't handle."

"You will treat those present with respect!" Everard grunted.

"Oh yes, respect from the very people that didn't respect me enough to invite me to this… sacred event?"

"Stop it with the smooth talk as nobody's buying it," Rikolf snapped. "You know very well that the reason you were not included is because *you* are the problem at hand, Lobjörn."

"Me? But I haven't done a thing."

"You have moved against Alexandria and Vermilion Bay," Warryn stated clearly. "Though there has been no violence…"

"Yet," added Rikolf.

Warryn shot him a cold stare before resuming. "Though there has been no violence, it is still in violation of the Treaty of Marksville – something signed by all of us many years ago. Need I cite the section?"

Lobjörn chuckled. "Damn you're a studious pigeon, aren't you? No, no I don't need the citation."

"Very well," Warryn said.

"Though, I do have a question," Lobjörn said. "Do you have to peck at people in order to turn them? However do you manage not to laugh?"

That was enough to send Rikolf bolting from his seat. He got to Lobjörn in a flash, grabbing him by the collar of his shirt and landing a blow to his face. The bear recoiled for a moment, grabbing Rikolf's wrists as he leaned in close to the bear's face. Both were trembling.

"I don't understand why you are doing this," Rikolf muttered. He was sweating. "But know that I will stand up to both you and these demons if necessary. We are strong."

Lobjörn let out a laugh, letting go of Rikolf's wrists but not before pushing them toward the wolf's own chest.

"Be careful what you wish for, little thing. One night something dark will come knocking, and you will be forced to answer the door."

Chapter 9

THE TRIO AT ODDS

Tuesday April 9, 2013

1

Alyssa poured herself a glass of iced tea from a pitcher, watching from the kitchen window as Billy and Cooper sat on the back porch of her house. They were talking about something, and it was getting heated; she could tell by their expressions even though the words were muffled under the sound of crackling ice.

I hope everything's alright between you two, she thought worriedly.

Ever since getting back from The Climb, Billy had been different. More to himself. Vacant. Alyssa didn't like that at all. It reminded her in some ways (a lot of ways, in fact) of her first encounter with Liam Manning back in 2001.

Just a shell wrapped around something angry and old…

Alyssa's mother, Amanda Noble, swanned into the room. Her high heels were ever clicking away on the hard floors. She was wearing a slimming dress, still selling luxury lake and mountainside properties out of her Clayton office.

Shouldn't you be gone by now? Alyssa wondered, but didn't ask.

"Good morning dear," Mrs. Noble said plainly, swooping in for a kiss on her daughter's cheek.

Alyssa obliged, even though she noticed her mother's hawkish gaze was now out toward the patio area.

That Bennett Boy again, Alyssa could read in her mother's countenance, *along with some new trash. Before long our home will be the start of a new North Goodman.*

Alyssa had hoped her parent's avoidance of impending death during Goodman's recent attacks would have spurred some kind of everlasting personality development. Sadly, any changes on the swankier side of town only lasted until the end of March, as if the new month meant it was time to shed the snake skin and be reborn an arrogant bitch once more.

"So, do you have any *constructive* plans for today dear?" asked Mrs. Noble as she stepped to the coffee machine, flicked it on, and waited.

Alyssa could swear her mother meant, "Are you going to be finding a decent boyfriend anytime soon?"

Alyssa spooled up an ample level of spritely cheer as she replied, "Nothing much today! Just planning to run around the woods like a pack of wild animals."

Mrs. Noble let an eyeroll slip past her defenses, quickly setting her mug down and starting the machine. It gurgled and belched water noisily. "I really wish you were still attending school."

"I would if they hadn't canceled it for the rest of the year. At least the seniors with good grades were granted immediate graduation."

"Yes, but we like to earn things, don't we?"

Alyssa about fell over, wondering if her mother had even heard the part about good grades. Besides, Mrs. Noble hadn't earned so much of anything recently, especially if it didn't involve some kind of elite social climbing, ass-kissery, or other nonsense. There wasn't a scrap of hard work done other than maintaining that wretched smile all day long.

"We sure do!" Alyssa said with a smile.

Longest. Coffee. Pour. Ever.

The pot finished spitting black tar into Mrs. Noble's white mug. She grabbed it and started for the door.

Alyssa was relieved until she paused again.

"You know," Mrs. Noble said. "I hope you're not becoming one of those…" and her voice dropped to a whisper, just in case someone was in earshot in Canada "… *goths*, are you?"

Alyssa let out a half-laugh. "Why… why on Earth would you think that?"

"Your hair dear. I miss the blonde. Whatever you're doing to it is far too dark."

"Um… thanks for the advice?"

"You know I worry about you dear."

Alyssa snatched her glass of sweet tea and headed for the door. She opened it, ominously saying, "Yes, and you should be worried Mother. Really worried." Then, like a crazed person she shifted tones and sprang out the rest of the way. "Okay bye now!"

As the door closed, Alyssa imagined that her mother was still staring at it, flabbergasted.

2

"So you're *still* planning on going to college?" Billy asked.

"Yes," Alyssa answered. "At least I think that's still something I can do. Right Cooper?"

"I… I think so," he replied. "After all, Liam was planning on it for football. Seems a pretty human thing to be doing."

Alyssa nodded and looked back to Billy with an *I told you* so expression on her face. He was seated on one of the Wolf's Ridge Greenway benches deep in thought. He looked vacant again.

"So… we still have to do those kinds of things?"

"For the times we're trying to interact with normal people, yes," Alyssa said.

"Or if you want things like *money*, Billy. Jesus, did you think that this would just be about lounging under the trees or frolicking in the mountains for the rest of our lives? You can't be that dumb."

That was kind of harsh Cooper, Alyssa thought. She started to get antsy, checking Billy's face for any dire signs.

"Of course I've thought about things, Cooper, but that doesn't make it any easier."

"And all the crap I've had to do and put up with has made my life a cakewalk?"

"Boys…" Alyssa said.

"Yeah but it's not like I've had a lot of time to adjust to this… condition." Billy was on his feet, stepping toward Cooper.

"I had to do all this shit on my own, brother. A lot of it." Cooper was edging his way toward Billy.

"Boys…"

"Oh, is Cooper Bennett upset he got blessed with *Alpha* powers? Or is he upset that his *shitty* father got killed?"

"You know, this is why nobody wants you around Billy! For fuck's sake, even your parents had the right idea to check out of town!"

"Cooper! Billy! Shut up! Now!"

They both stopped at once, gazing at Alyssa with bulging eyes. She had moved to the water's edge and was holding a rock in each hand. Throwing them as hard as she could, each struck her target in the legs, and they keeled over in pain.

"What the hell was that for?" Cooper yelled.

"Just physically manifesting the crap you two are throwing at each other," she snipped. "Now quit it! This is not the time to let whatever damn pressure is building get between us. You two are better than this!"

Billy sighed, more because his leg hurt than any respect he had for Cooper at that moment.

"Billy, are you okay?" Alyssa asked.

"Yeah," he replied, "but that is quite a throwing arm you have."

"Helped dating a football player for so long," Alyssa said, not caring if Cooper was upset. He'd get over it.

Alyssa was growing concerned about Billy though, his presence was going to cause issues amongst all the wolves eventually. Even though the Shadow Wolves seemed amicable then, they wouldn't stay that way forever.

Does he have to leave? Can he stay? What about our promises? Our family? Alyssa didn't know the answer to any of the questions, and that scared her to death and back again.

"I'm not sure what's going on in your head right now, Billy," she told him, "but please, don't put up walls to keep us out."

Billy got to his feet, hobbled a moment, then made his way to the bench again. "Look, I know what you guys are trying to do for me, and I appreciate it a lot."

"Billy…"

"But I can tell that you guys don't want me around."

"That's not true at all! Cooper, say something."

Cooper was quiet, looking out to the creek.

"See?" Billy said. "It's tough to want to be around a loser when you're a winner. Besides, I… I don't think I can be around the things that killed my parents. It's just too hard a thing to swallow."

Alyssa was in tears; Cooper still silent.

What are you doing Cooper? her mind screamed at him.

Billy reached for the chain around his neck, pulling out the white ring from under his tank top.

Alyssa tried to say something, anything, to stop him but the words were stuck behind those tears.

Billy removed the chain, lifting it over his head. Balling up the chain and ring in his fist, he held it close to his heart for a second, then threw it into the bushes. "I'm going to head home," he said somberly. "Don't bother coming."

Alyssa watched helplessly as Billy turned and marched north along the walking path. She sat there the entire time he was in view, then even longer once he was not. Hearing scuffling, she looked over toward Cooper, who had finally gotten up to his feet.

She ran toward him, angry as Hell, but didn't say anything. She just stood there hugging Cooper and crying.

"You going to be okay?" he asked eventually.

"I don't think so," she answered. "What about him? You think he is going to be ok?"

"I… I want to say yes but he's... different now, isn't he?"

"You are too," she added. "We all are."

Cooper hugged her, stepped back, then approached the bushes Billy tossed the ring into. After a brief search he found it, clinging to the branches of a tiny sapling. Picking it up, Cooper walked back to Alyssa and started to put it over her neck. She stopped him, putting it around his own neck instead.

2

After a few moments of silence in that breezy Greenway, Cooper started to sniffle. He pulled away from Alyssa, managing to keep tears from spilling over what had just happened.

"Baby, I had another one of the dreams last night. I… I think it's what put me in such a shit mood today."

"It's been a while since the last one you had," she said understandingly, though part of her wished he could have pushed through and not blown up at Billy. "I thought it might have been getting better. What was it about?"

Cooper elaborated, describing things that put him in awe – like magnificent flying creatures straight out of legends, as well as things that petrified him.

"Torture with kitchen utensils?" she said. "That sounds horrific!"

"I know, and I wish that was the last of it."

He went on to mention a dark cabin in the woods.

"And there were these creepy noises, like low cackling and something like nails scraping across the floor."

Alyssa's skin pebbled like gooseflesh.

"I also saw a trio of figures opposite this massive army…"

"Us?" she asked.

"I don't think so," Cooper said. "Even though I couldn't see their faces they seemed older than we were. Not by much. I can't explain it, but that's what I felt."

"Any more details?"

"Yeah," Cooper said. "There was this dark figure that emerged from the masses. There was a flaming crown on his head, and his eyes glowed with the deepest red color."

"Sounds demonic," Alyssa said, "based on what I know about demons. Which isn't much."

"I think that's exactly what they were. But the worst part of it?"

"Worst part?"

"They seemed to notice me," he said. "It's like they know I'm there."

A chill descended down both of their spines, intensified when the two suddenly heard a distant howl. It was above the sound of wind in the trees and birds calling.

"Billy?" Alyssa asked.

"No, that's far too somber."

Alyssa looked away. "Then it's time isn't it?"

"The time we were waiting for yet dreading?"

Alyssa nodded. "Seems to be our way of life at the moment."

"Well, this will close one chapter of our lives at least. Hopefully for the better."

"That's true but I wonder what the rest of the story has in store."

Cooper was quiet as they both walked back toward town, and Alyssa didn't say another word, knowing that deep down beneath his confident exterior, Cooper felt the same amount of dread she did, if not more.

Chapter 10

A MAN POSSESSED

1

Earlier that Tuesday morning and several states away, a small, wooden shed was shrouded in fog. A few hours from then, the property would resume its appearance as an unassuming bit of land bordering Bayou Macon, just off LA-577. However, the current blanket of gray changed things, adding an eeriness to the sinister shapes that moved through the veil. Men became monsters, and monsters, well they became true nightmares.

A shadowed form emerged from the dark woods close to the shed, skulking its way across the dewy grass to a door. The large slab of rusted metal looked more designed for a prison (to keep dangerous things in), rather than one for storing garden tools (unless vintage lawn mowers were known for their ability to escape). The figure fidgeted with a lock, and after a few bangs and screeches, the door was open and it was inside.

Lobjörn bowed as he entered, then stood taller to look around the grimy place, which was indeed more for detaining than storage. There were no mowers or other large pieces of equipment there, just cobwebs all around, some general tools that had seen better days, and, in the center, a cage.

Having left The Gathering triumphantly (his main resistance Rikolf – who had managed to land quite the heavy punch on his face before Lobjörn sent him crashing into the courtyard's fountain), there was a fire in the crazed bear's eyes, flickering like the tiny light was in the right corner of the room.

He stared madly at the cage. It was tall, thin, and round, with bands of spiked iron that were spaced wide enough to grab through, but not bodily escape. Inside was a man, naked and bruised; the same one that had been captured in late March trying to escape with a kingly prize. *His* prize.

"How are we tonight, demon?" Lobjörn asked loftily. "Are the new accommodations satisfactory?"

The demon glanced at, then studied the bruise on Lobjörn's face with his red eyes. Though healing, traces of it were still visible. "My night wasn't as good as yours was by the looks of things. As for the accommodations, I've stayed in better. Maybe some curtains not made of spider webs could brighten the place up."

A short and low laugh came from Lobjörn as he walked toward the cage, stopping at a pegboard beforehand.

"I have more *questions* for you demon," he said, plucking a pair of pruning shears from the display.

"You *know* my name," the creature hissed. "I recall you 'asked' me what it was for quite a while. The least you could do, Your 'Eminence', is use it."

Lobjörn tapped the blades of the shears against his head in thinking. "Ah, yes, Camio wasn't it?"

The demon exhaled.

"You seemed awfully intent on keeping that from me for some reason. I hope tonight goes a little better – I have some other things to do."

"Can't your lap dog Hægen take care of that for you? Or is he too busy finding his way out of your –"

Lobjörn smashed a hand against the cage. It made a tremendous noise. During the distraction, the Bear King grabbed the demon's arms, brought them forward, and touched them to the iron bands of the cage.

Camio screamed; his skin sizzled, and Lobjörn smiled.

Releasing the demon after a full, grueling minute of burning, Lobjörn cleared the smoke from his eyes, coughed once, then said, "So, back to our last discussion about these 'Solomon Seals.' They seem quite powerful, and by that, I mean useful."

Camio nodded grudgingly. "Yes, but demons have no use for those damnable symbols. Our kind uses runes instead."

"Ah, I see. From what I remember some can even control your kind. Anyway, these symbols and runes can just be drawn on anything and *poof* they work?"

"Yes," Camio muttered, touching his burns with his fingertips. "Though they must be exactly reproduced."

"Show me one," Lobjörn demanded.

"Did you not hear me? They must be precise to work!"

Lobjörn snatched Camio's arm again (it was sticky) and squeezed. "Do an easy one then. Must I do *all* the thinking for you?"

"What… what shall I draw with? Does Hægen have a pencil with him up there?"

Lobjörn pressed his thumb into Camio's forearm, blood oozing out of the bubbling skin. "No, but ask and you shall receive."

Camio was free again, but not from pain. Dipping a shaky finger into the blood, he crouched, then started drawing on the floor.

"Don't even think to draw something that will help you escape," Lobjörn said strictly, thinking a symbol like that would be too complex.

Camio drew a simple arrow with two finger strokes; it was pointed to the left.

"That's it? What is it?"

"It is Kenaz, Rune of Fire," Camio answered weakly. "The easiest one that came to mind."

"Why is it just sitting there if you've drawn it accurately?"

Camio dropped his voice to a mumbling whisper. "It needs both air to breathe life into the symbol and energy to unleash the power." He knew what was coming next.

"Show me."

Camio hesitated.

"SHOW ME!" Lobjörn roared, bashing the side of the cage again.

Camio, still on his knees, bent over more, placing his lips above the symbol. With a quivering breath he blew across it. The rune awakened, sparking between its bloody lines as the demon raised one of his hands high, only to bring it crashing down on the symbol.

There was an explosion of color and screams, Lobjörn watching with absolute delight. "Magnificent…"

As the light faded, so did Camio's wails. Burned and battered, the demon – in a way – looked pathetic and sad. Lobjörn knew better than to trust it, or feel for it, or care.

"So," he continued without rest. "The rumors have your army moving west; toward here it would seem. Why?"

Camio hissed and sputtered, but he said no words.

"Tsk, tsk," Lobjörn said. "I thought we were going to be more cooperative tonight. I had considered getting you those curtains you so wanted."

Reaching into the cage, Lobjörn grabbed Camio's hand (the one that had impacted the rune), ignoring the struggling demon as he drew it outside of the cage. He placed the shears at the tip of one of Camio's fingers, digging the lower blade into the nail bed as the upper blade hovered above the plate.

"What are you seeking? Is it the amulet?"

Camio glared at him, expression blank.

The blades connected in one swift motion, then moved to the next finger.

"Is. It. This?"

Breathing heavily, teeth clenched, Camio nodded. "We… seek… the artifacts…"

"Why?"

"To… open a door… home."

"Trying to get back there?" Lobjörn pressed for answers. When they didn't come fast enough, he cut again, then moved to the next finger.

By now Camio was incensed. Breathless with snot pouring from his nose, the edges of his dark and crimson eyes were like rivers of soiled water. "No… you fool… to bring what is there… here."

"We shall see," countered Lobjörn confidently. "You mentioned artifacts, as if there are more than one."

"You possess two…"

"How many more are there?"

Camio braced himself for the cut. Lobjörn delivered.

"There are six in all…" a weak demon answered, then laughed. "You are in way over your head, bear. The Devil's Ire and its Shackles belong to the Great Demon himself!"

"How fortuitous it is then that such a mighty gift has come into my possession." Lobjörn was cocky. "The tide is certainly turning."

"Fortune… had… nothing to do with this. An error brought the amulet to your swamp."

"An error?" Lobjörn asked, sniggering. "The Devil isn't so 'Great' then, is he?"

"Blasphemy!" Camio yelled with renewed strength. "But it is not Lucifer of whom I speak. Dajjal is his name."

"Well, whoever that is will have to pry this amulet from my cold, dead hands."

"That can be arranged," Camio replied, a sharp scream following as a fourth finger was split by those warm, metal blades.

Chapter 11

CLOSING A CHAPTER OF THE PAST

1

The sun scaled the sky above Goodman, Cooper and Alyssa arriving at Bower's Funeral home on the west side of town around eleven o'clock. As the Acura RL slowed, then came to a stop, Cooper looked at the one story building with its long, beige bricks, then over to Alyssa, who was sitting in the driver's seat.

"Are you ready for this?" he asked her, knowing the amount of time she had spent with Liam (even though it was not the best of times).

She nodded loosely. "How about you?"

Before replying, Cooper thought back on all the times Liam had bullied him. Then, he hated the guy and all his smugness, Daddy Manning bucks falling out of his pockets to pay any and everyone around to look the other way. Yet, now that Liam was… gone… and that Cooper had witnessed his demise by six silver bullets in the bowels of the Vault, there was sort of a poetic finality to the entire thing, and Cooper found himself to be much more sad than mad.

"I think I'm going to be okay," he replied. "Come on, let's go."

The two of them exited the car, met up at the front of it, and interlocked arms. Alyssa had changed into a black outfit; a simple dress and a rose-adorned wide-brimmed hat with matching shoes. Cooper wore a crisp dress shirt, unbuttoned, and dark pants that Alyssa had insisted she get him for more formal occasions. That day was the first time he'd worn any of it.

Beyond the funeral home, which faced south, Cooper could see the mountains of Toluca Springs National Forest rising up in irony – for there he was, standing in the shadow of the place that started his new life, while the person that set that life in motion was at the end of theirs, inside the building ahead.

Reaching the door, Cooper opened it and Alyssa passed through silently. They entered a carpeted lobby (neutral in tone like the brick outside), and were directed to the right by one of the funeral attendants. The stocky man had unnaturally blue eyes, and Cooper knew instantly that he was one of the White Wolves. On their way, Cooper and Alyssa passed by several office doors, all closed, noting paintings of landscapes from Germany between each. Before long they had reached a set of double mahogany doors. To the left of it was a sign that simply said MANNING.

Alyssa paused. Cooper hugged her.

"You don't have to go," he said.

"No," she replied softly. "We have to."

Cooper told her it would be okay, kissed her cheek, then moved to pull one of the doors open; it was heavy like his restless heart. Alyssa entered first again with Cooper falling in behind.

The first thing that struck him was the fragrance that filled the room, a luscious floral scent that managed to set him at ease. Then he saw an abundance of white and blue standing sprays and wreaths, all brimming with lush greenery, lilies, carnations, and studded with blue delphinium. At last Cooper's eyes fell on the closed casket – white with silver accents – and things grew dark. The only light came from the two snow-white rose displays set on the casket's lid, their satin ribbons entwined with a tiny stuffed wolf sitting upright between them. Cooper felt incredibly sad, weighed down by helplessness and guilt.

What if we could have helped Liam down in the Vault?

What if we could have helped Lance there, too?

The burden of "what ifs" was overbearing, able to sink even the mightiest resolve, and Cooper knew that his future would be full of "what ifs" for many years to come.

Like, *What if Billy never comes back?*

The room brightened again, and Cooper moved to sit with Alyssa near the back of the room. As he sat, he saw Liam's senior photo on display to the far right. He looked handsome and happy. Below his picture was his name, and the dates January 5, 1994 – March 16, 2013.

Cooper had spoken briefly with Grayson a week or so ago and discovered the ceremony was going to happen. The Order had at last recovered Liam's body from the Vault. Cooper suspected they'd done so more to recover the items inside than to help a shifter – even one as obedient as Grayson – get his son's body back.

Either way, Grayson was thankful which is what mattered, but Cooper believed the Order was also in trouble. The expediency with which they managed to open, drain, and extract items from the Vault was *too* fast, leading him to think their encounters with the rumored demons Lance mentioned were not going well.

A haunting melody drew Cooper's mind back to the funeral home. *Ave Maria* was being played on a piano, and was soon joined by soft and distant howls in the mountain.

Grayson then stood, making his way for the middle of the room. He was still an attractive, middle-aged man, regal but a little more worn around the eyes. His hair had always been white like a fresh snowfall, but to Cooper it seemed less vibrant than before. Grayson stopped at the stuffed animal, picked it up, and said, "I bought this toy a month before Liam was born. Freya, my dear Freya, thought that I was insane – my level of excitement in meeting him was immeasurable. It was one of only a few things that survived the fire Lance set in the safe house back in 1994. Freya did not make it, as you know, but Liam and this did. Fast forward to now and Liam is gone… murdered… but this toy survived the manor fires also started by Lance. Funny that, isn't it? As happy as this toy made me waiting for Liam to be born, I'd much rather my boy still be around, and that we wouldn't have to be standing here today."

Alyssa quietly sobbed. Cooper wrapped an arm around her as he did too.

"For all my financial success," Grayson continued, "I failed as a husband, a father, and a protector. I think that ultimately sent Liam on his path of unruliness, affecting more people that I ever knew. That is, until one boy… one man… opened my eyes. Cooper, I am sorry for what Liam did to you and your friends. I apologize that he brought you, unknowing and unwilling, into this strange life. I apologize that I didn't see it before, and that I can't return all the time and energy lost, but I promise that I will help you however I can now. From one Alpha to another: thank you."

Grayson looked to have more to say, but did not. He moved back toward his seat as the melody faded and another began.

Cooper rose, Alyssa wondering if he was planning to leave. Instead, Cooper made his way to the front of the room. He set a single hand on the cold casket, then moved it to the bouquet closest to him, where the gentle petals caressed his skin.

"Mr. Manning… Grayson… you have nothing to apologize for, especially to me. Liam made his own decisions given the fantastic life you afforded him – trust me that not everyone is or was so blessed with what they were dealt. Some of us had nothing but belts and fists to look forward to as "thank yous" and "you're welcomes" all wrapped up in nice, tight packages. Though his actions may have stemmed from his past, Liam followed them of his own accord, and all of it – every single second – had already been set in motion by Lance Goddard and his misguided actions."

Grayson's blue eyes watered, falling to his son's casket, and Cooper could actually feel his loss for not only Liam, but his brother Lance.

Cooper turned to Liam's photo and said, "Thank you, and also to you Lance, for shaping me into the person… the man… the beast that I am today. Without you, I wouldn't have formed such solid bonds of friendship (he thought of Billy), and family (*Alyssa… Grayson…*), and I will carry those bonds, along with the people they are connected to for the rest of my life."

As Cooper turned, his eyes grew wide, and once again he was crying right in front of everyone. Sitting next to Alyssa at the back of the room was Billy, who had snuck in during the speech. At last, Cooper's heart managed to find some peace.

2

Wednesday April 10, 2013

The next night, under its moonless sky, Cooper walked up to the Greyhound bus station off Foothill Road. He thought it was an odd place for Grayson to want to meet, but he did regardless, vaguely recalling himself running up from there in a panic to escape Liam and his thugs, then somehow making it back from the mountains alive, but bitten and beaten.

Grayson was seated on a bench beneath the shelter, head down and holding a picture of his mate, Freya, who in turn was holding a cute baby Liam in her arms.

"Ah, Cooper," he said, having obviously just finished an emotional spell. "It's good to see you. Wonderful night, isn't it?"

Cooper nodded, saying, "There's no moon."

"Exactly," Grayson replied. "It's nice to escape that bond every now and then and just be… alive."

Cooper sat beside him; Grayson put the picture away and gave a sigh.

"So why'd you ask to see me?" Cooper questioned.

"I have been thinking," Grayson said. "Quite a bit since I have a lot of time on my hands at the moment."

Cooper started to feel a little uneasy.

"You remember Ásbjörn, right? Our lumbering bear friend."

"Of course."

"He never returned to this area after the Journeymen called him up to their headquarters in New York. He just… left. No idea where, but that's exactly what he did."

Cooper's stomach started twisting in a long, slow knot.

"I think I need to do the same. Obviously I can't go where he has… haha… but somewhere… else."

Cooper didn't know what to say, witnessing how lost Grayson truly felt while Cooper seemed to be gaining direction with his life, even though he knew significant hurdles were still in the way.

"Grayson," Cooper said in return. "I… I don't think that's such a good idea."

"Why is that?" Grayson asked, his eyes hopeful.

"Well, first, you did promise me that you'd help in the future. I've no idea how that'd be possible if you weren't here. And if not for me, then for our packs and this new relationship. What is yours going to do without your level of leadership at the helm? I think the both of us owe that to the wolves who remained loyal to us and our ideals after the battle in 1994 and this most recent one."

Grayson exhaled sharply, then grinned. "You truly are wise beyond your age, Cooper. Which is a good thing, because it's not going to get any easier. From one Alpha to another: the true test of your resolve hasn't even started yet."

"As you said, we are all a product of our past," he replied, "and mine's been a shit show, until now. Until I met you and gained a role model."

Grayson's eyes shimmered, his grin growing slightly. "I appreciate that Cooper, far more than you realize."

Suddenly, the two heard a rush of air that sounded like flapping. Standing quickly and searching, they couldn't see anything in the darkness that quickly engulfed their views beyond the bus shelter.

"Who's there?" Cooper asked, lowering his arms, ready to transform. *Why does the threat of shifting always come around when I'm wearing my favorite shirt?* he thought.

"Show yourself!" Grayson commanded, and out of the night emerged a woman dressed in flowing robes. She had on large, feathered earrings that framed her face in gold.

Cooper was lost as he took in the sight, but Grayson seemed taken aback when she spoke.

"I have been sent from Vermilion Bay," she said hurriedly, Cajun accent heavy. "We are in need of your help."

"What's happened?" Grayson asked, and when she did not answer right away his voice suddenly boomed. Anger filled the bus station, echoing into the mountain along with his next words. "Tell me, dammit! Tell me now!"

Chapter 12

VERMILION BAY RUNS RED

Wednesday April 10, 2013

1

Near midday on Wednesday, the wolf shifters of Vermilion Bay, residing at Cypremort Point, were going about their daily lives. Similar to the situation in Goodman, though on a much smaller scale, the citizens appeared outwardly as normal townsfolk since settling in the area after being driven west by the vampires of the Germain Coven so many years ago.

Rikolf was walking the streets like he normally did every day, passing tall grass edging the rough pavement, to check on things and

make sure all was in order. This time he was joined by Warryn –
who had been tending to Rikolf (and his temper) since Monday night
and their incident with Lobjörn.

"I can't believe he just got away!" Rikolf said, kicking a stray
stone into the marshes off Bayouview Drive. It didn't bounce,
instead sinking immediately like Rikolf's mood.

"I too would have loved to have seen him incarcerated," Warryn
said in his typically stoic manner, "but I think we all sensed
something… off about him."

"Yeah, I know exactly what you mean. It was like…" Rikolf
started, a quizzical looked spreading across his face. He couldn't
figure out how to describe it.

"Like he was possessed by power?" Warryn offered as a
suggestion.

To that Rikolf nodded, unsure how else to put it, and if the bird
couldn't get it right, no one could.

The two continued along the road southward. Cypremort meant
"dead Cyprus," and many that would look at the settlement would
likely judge its appearance as befitting that name. It was admittedly
very easy to; the residences were plain at their best, junky at their
worst. Most of the wooden homes along the water's edge had
rickety, jutting piers that shot offshore like the legs of a juvenile
whirligig beetle. Vermilion Bay spread itself to the west, with Bayou

Cypremort to the north, and West Cote Blanche Bay toward the south and east.

As Rikolf looked around, he knew that they lived a simple (and poor) life, but he and his pack were happy. There were only a few businesses in the immediate area – a seafood retailer and market, yacht club, some quaint shops, and an inn. Cypremort State Park was also to the northeast, bringing in new faces periodically, especially those who liked the wilderness, boating, and fishing. Yet, as Rikolf also knew, despite the simplicity their lives afforded, there were issues that came up, some far too often.

"I'm sorry if my mood has been edgy, Warryn."

"Edgy would be an understatement, my friend, *but* fully understandable with all things considered."

Rikolf paused outside one of the shops; it sold beachy crafts. Finding a spot on its weathered and blue-painted walls, Rikolf leaned against it. Crossed his arms.

Warryn approached too, considering several wind chimes made with shells that were hanging on a display. They were pretty, and swayed gently in the breeze, but the sounds they made weren't appealing at all.

"This situation with the Tensas Bears is aggravating!"

Warryn stayed silent, and listened.

"You know, I never wanted this position as Alpha," Rikolf continued, kicking a leg up and dropping a beating fist to his side, "but it was kind of thrown at me after *Far* was killed."

It had happened a year ago that March, his Father (Alpha at the time), was killed by a human. It was immense luck on that hunter's part that his shot landed right where it needed to – between his eyes – to end him instantly.

"That stigma's stuck on me like shit on a boar's ass. It makes me feel like everything – and I mean *everything* – is spinning a slow and painful death around a drain. No matter what I try to do, I'm destined to get pulled down into those depths and never succeed."

"Plus, your lack of retaliation against the humans didn't help matters in the eyes of your subordinates."

"No, it didn't," Rikolf stated plainly. "It's just not my way."

"You could have fooled me with how you've been handling the issues with Lobjörn! I'd have thought it was your *only* way, if I didn't know you better."

"Consider me… unpredictable," Rikolf chuckled.

"Well, despite all that unpredictability, you'll endure," Warryn said comfortingly, and Rikolf appreciated it.

The reluctant Alpha kicked off from the wall, continuing down the street.

"You hungry?" he asked Warryn, and since they both were he made way for the seafood market. They often had fresh food available for purchase.

What the two did not discuss along their way was the proverbial elephant in the room. It was Rikolf's lack of a mate, which was likely the largest wedge driven in the middle of the pack. The only thing saving him from a complete overthrow was the fear of both the rumored demon army and, recently, Lobjörn.

A short time later Rikolf and Warryn arrived at the market. Their stomachs growled in approval as they saw picnic tables set up nearby, along with bubbling pots above open fires. Inside were various fruits of the sea, each delicious in mind and even more in belly.

"Ah, welcome my Alpha!" said the kind voice of the proprietor, a stout shifter no taller than four and a half feet. He wore a chef's hat that was nearly as tall as he was. "I have a seafood boil coming right up! It's just become ready!"

As Rikolf and Warryn sat down to enjoy their upcoming meal, from the east came the sounds of a large scuffle, then screaming as citizens began to flee in a panic. Vermilion Bay appeared to be under attack in some form, and it didn't take long to guess who the culprit was.

"And so it begins," Warryn said calmly.

"It began long before today!" Rikolf's tone was in opposition to Warryn's.

The Alpha removed his vest and pants quickly, lobbing them in a wad on the picnic table. His body began to bend and groan, the sounds of his bones breaking and reforming were unpleasant as he transformed into a ruddy wolf. The runes etched along the inner edge of his nose ring allowed it to grow twice as large, still set in place once his Change had ended.

Similarly Warryn stood, and with arms outstretched, his dark skin seemed to quake while his robes did not rip nor tear, instead they transformed *with* him into large feathers. His neck cracked and his face grew long and beak-like, before long a large eagle taking its place beside Rikolf.

In the shade of a nearby grouping of trees, Rikolf saw some of his pack – a woman and child still in human form – trying to escape. Two other wolf shifters ran toward them and Rikolf's heart lifted as he would see them helped. However, his soul crashed through the ground when he saw what happened next, as flesh met claws and teeth within a spray of red. He could not believe it; the wolves were reddish brown in color. They were from *his own pack!*

"What is this treachery?" he whispered, then howled frantically as he charged the rebels.

Warryn spread his wings wide and took off at once, following Rikolf's path toward the pair of attacking wolves.

"How… dare… you!" Rikolf roared, and with thunderous paws he leaped at the wolf closest to him, plowing into its side with his ringed muzzle.

Wheezing, they both hit the ground hard, then rolled. Rikolf was on his feet in a flash, long before the other wolf could recover. Then, with his jaws planted firmly on the base of the traitor's neck, he clamped down and twisted sharply until it snapped. Letting go, the wolf collapsed to the ground a dead heap, and Rikolf rushed to the woman and child to see if they were okay.

Meanwhile, the other wolf had spotted Warryn and ran, trying to lose him under the cover of the trees. However, Warryn was skilled while the subordinate was not, easily darting between the branches at speed. Seeing his chance, like a falcon eyeing its prey, Warryn dove while screaming, talons out and ready. He dug them into the wolf's back. Though heavy, Warryn banked, then soared skyward, target wriggling yet still held firm. Passing the tree line, he rose higher and higher, garnering a full view of the Bay and seeing that this was not an isolated attack. It was far worse. Releasing his quarry, the treacherous wolf plummeted toward the ground, striking it head first with a karmic *thud*.

Rikolf was looking over the bodies of the two victims when Warryn arrived, trying not to weep at the blood-covered sight. The eagle landed beside the wolf, taking in the carnage for himself.

"Rikolf, it is worse than just these two. The entire area has been attacked. Coming from the east through the marshes."

"What?"

"I could not tell how much damage has been done, but…" a sudden sound of trees falling and many footsteps running cut in to the conversation, "we have to fight, and get help."

"Agreed," Rikolf said. "Send word to the few wolves still around New Orleans to meet us at the State Park, though I need you to get a priority message to the Blue Ridge Mountains."

"That is a long way to ask for aid," Warryn pointed out.

"Favors don't know boundaries," Rikolf replied, "and neither does family."

"Very well," Warryn said, "will you be okay to get out of here?"

Rikolf nodded. "No worries, I've got this."

Warryn rose quickly, shooting toward the sky with an intense screech. Calling to all the birds residing in the forest and beyond, the Leader of the Aves told them all to get help, and that the time to do so was short.

Part Two: Objects in Motion

Chapter 13

NEW PERSPECTIVES

Wednesday April 10, 2013

1

Alyssa and Billy followed Cooper inside what was left of Grayson Manor, the term "inside" a loose one since the building's skeletal remains more resembled the jagged bones of some long-dead monster than one of the most luxurious homes in town. He had caught the both of them up on what was going on, at least as much as he knew about the situation, which had grown quite frantic.

"I wonder why there are no rebuild efforts underway?" Alyssa asked as they passed through what was once the front door, traveling through a once ornate lobby, down a short hallway, ending at Grayson's former office.

"I'm not sure, maybe he's been tied up with Order," Cooper replied. He hadn't told either of them about Grayson's plans to leave; there was no need.

Billy moved toward a sofa, situated in front of a blackened fireplace, while Alyssa approached a section of unburnt wall toward the broken windows. The decorative paneling was still exquisite as if freshly polished, and there was a lingering scent of citrus oil under all the char.

Unexpectedly, Grayson emerged from a cubbyhole that was on the other side of Alyssa. She gasped, tumbling backwards into Cooper's waiting arms.

Grayson was hurriedly packing a case the size of an airline carry-on bag, paying them little, if any, attention. He was wearing a pair of blue jeans and a white tee shirt beneath a leather jacket. The look was completely different, something none of them were used to. All they had seen him in before were designer suits, shirts, and shoes. Cooper wouldn't be surprised if the attire he had on was designer too.

"What's going on, Mr. Manning?" Alyssa asked warily.

"Frosty seems awfully distracted," Billy said, then waited for some sign of irritation or rage. "Guess he likes that nickname."

Grayson had been visibly and mentally preoccupied ever since the arrival of the avian emissary from Vermilion Bay. After receiving word of the trouble, they beelined for the manor with little to say, Cooper calling Alyssa and Billy over right away.

"Grayson," Cooper vied for his attention. "Grayson!"

"You won't get much out of him until he is ready to go," the avian shifter interrupted. She explained the situation in more detail to the trio – from the mounting tension between the clans of Louisiana, to demons, to the most recent attacks.

"Thank you for that," Alyssa said, fascinated by both the stories and the Cajun dialect.

"This is all well and good," Cooper added, "but I'm still lost. And forgive me if I seem forward, but how can we trust you? I don't even have a name."

The shifter paused. She bowed formally. "My name is Theryn, and I am Leader of Peveto Woods."

"What a pleasure," Billy said graciously, then, once that was out of the way his tone changed back to normal. "What is it with all the shifters and these weird names? Theryn, Ásbjörn, *Low-ja-born...*"

"Low-born," Theryn corrected with a smile, "though the spelling *is* the challenge with that one."

"Yeah," Billy continued. "I feel like I'm at a fantasy convention – and trust me I love fantasy – but *damn!* I can barely say my own name on a good day. I'm good at faces though. Um, human faces... not animals. Everyone looks the same when shifted too." He glanced around the room, noticing the dark hair on everyone except Grayson. "Um, no offense."

"Hmmm," Cooper said, sitting cockeyed in one of the armchairs. "On the demons, I remember Lance making some offhand remark about their army coming. That was back in January."

Grayson paused, the mention of Lance seeming to snap him to some level of mindfulness.

"He did the same with me as far back as October," Grayson said. "I was in no mood to listen to anything he had to say at that time, thinking it a distraction instead of a wider picture."

"Same," Cooper stated, his eyes on Alyssa, then Billy. That was when Lance had threatened to kill the two of them if he didn't succumb and join the Shadow Wolves as a subordinate.

"What is it?" Billy said anxiously. "Have I got something in my teeth?"

"No... it's nothing at all," Cooper replied. "Which is a *good* thing brother."

"How would Lance know anything about demons?" Alyssa asked Grayson.

"My brother traveled a lot after leaving Goodman in the early 1900s, so he could have easily picked up on whispers and trails from just about anywhere in the south. He ended up in Louisiana for a time; a long time. I even visited him there despite our growing separation and… met new people."

Grayson's eyes looked to his pocket. Cooper knew that was where he stowed the photo of Freya and baby Liam. "So, this level of urgency to go isn't just because of demons, is it?"

Grayson stopped packing at once and slumped in the only chair left unoccupied.

"No, it isn't," he said somberly. "You see, my wife Freya was a she-wolf from the southern clans. Specifically, Vermilion Bay."

Theryn nodded. "Rikolf is their Alpha, the one requesting aid".

"Now see, *that's* a cool name," Billy adds. "I like the sound of that."

"Only because you can say it," Alyssa jabbed.

"Freya was his older sister," Grayson continued. "We were bound in marriage in those many years before Liam was born, a way of uniting our packs, our species, during what would certainly be difficult times."

Alyssa was enjoying this sort of alternate history lesson, despite the severity of things attached to it. "What sort of difficulties?"

"Hunters, mainly," Theryn told her, "and other monsters. The wolves were deep in their conflict with the vampires of the area for many years. Unfortunately, we didn't know that the Order should be on that list too. We all learned that the world is a dangerous place, even if united against the evil in it."

"Sounds like Louisiana is getting high on that list of dangerous places," said Cooper.

"It always has been," Theryn said, her voice low.

"Which is exactly why I should be there," Grayson said.

"You mean *us*."

"No," Grayson snapped. "No, Cooper. This is my problem, not yours. I'm supposed to be helping you, remember, not bringing more troubles in your direction. Besides, you have the Shadow Wolves to deal with now…"

"Those issues can wait," Cooper said. "Consider it Alpha's choice. You're family Grayson, so you need to start understanding that fact. You aren't going alone."

Grayson stayed silent.

"It'll give us a chance to see what else is out there," Alyssa added. "Which will help us and the pack long term. Lifelong learning after all."

"See," Cooper agreed. "Can't argue with learning!"

"Not to be a bother," Billy said, "But Grayson originally was planning to go this alone."

"Yeah…" Cooper replied.

"So now that there's a ton more people going, how are we going to get there quickly?"

Theryn shrugged. "Do you have a car?" she asked. "I'm not carrying you all across country on my back."

"Alyssa does," Billy volunteered.

"Um, yes, yes I do."

"That will take too long," Grayson said. "But, I may have just the thing." After a snap of his fingers, he headed to a reinforced safe that was in the cubbyhole he'd emerged from earlier. He returned a few minutes later (after the sounds of a metric ton of paper rifling and several things falling over), holding a fist-sized stone etched with markings.

"What's that?" Billy asked like a kid on Christmas.

"It's called a transportation stone," Grayson said. "The Order use them all the time to move their Elite Operatives and Councilors around."

"How'd you get that?" Theryn asked as she stepped away from the group. "I think I'll make my way back the old-fashioned way."

"I might have gotten it from the Vault," Grayson stated. "Somehow…"

Cooper chuckled.

"Wait, you aren't coming with us?" Billy asked Theryn.

"No," she replied speedily.

"Why?"

"Because I don't feel like having my insides torn out and then stuffed back in again."

Cooper and Alyssa eyed each other nervously. The car sounded like a really good option now.

"Cool!" Billy exclaimed. "Makes me wonder what else the Order has access to!"

"I don't know if I want to know," Cooper said. Then a thought struck him hard. "Oh! Before I forget like I have already!"

He removed the chain from his neck and the white ring dangled on it. He handed it to Billy. "I was so emotional at the funeral I forgot to give this back to you. It's… just in case things go bad… not that I want them to go bad… but… I wanted you to have this back."

Billy took hold of it, held it against his chest, held back the tears. "Thank you, brother."

"I shall see you there, Grayson," Theryn said as she departed.

"Sounds good, and safe travels to you," Grayson replied. "Okay you three, gather around me and place your hands on each other's shoulders. Cooper, place your other hand on mine. Come now, quickly!"

The ABCs did what Grayson instructed, forming a tight but sort of lopsided square with their adjoined hands.

The silver-haired man looked to the floor, sighing. It was cracked, broken, and singed – the obvious memory of its former glory in his mind. "Well, at least I won't have to worry about cleaning up this extra damage. Ready?"

Grayson lifted the stone above his head, waited a moment.

"Three…"

Cooper felt an overwhelming urge to pee. It came out of nowhere but he had to hold it.

"Two…"

Cooper shut his eyes and readied himself for what would surely be one uncomfortable ride.

"One!"

Grayson threw the stone hard toward the floor, shattering it. Instantly, a whoosh of cold air enveloped them and with a swift, piercing *pop*, all four vanished without a trace.

Hopefully, they were already breathing the Louisiana air…

Chapter 14

FROM GEORGIA WITH LOVE

Thursday April 11, 2013

1

Cooper felt his feet hit the unyielding ground first, though it might have been his arms, or maybe his back. He had no idea which way was up or down, inside or out, though his stomach was doing its best to bring out everything he'd eaten for the last two days for the world to see. Billy bumped into him as he staggered by, trying his best not to lose his lunch either. Alyssa on the other hand seemed fine, now sitting with her legs crossed as if she'd been meditating for hours, except her unbridled hair told a completely different story about what she had just experienced.

Grayson was nowhere to be seen, Cooper wondering if he was alright. He couldn't hide the look on his face if he wanted to.

"He's okay," Alyssa said consolingly. "*Remarkably* okay to be honest. It's like he just walked into a different room while we were… less capable."

Cooper belched as Alyssa mentioned he'd gone on to the main camp to check on things. He could taste pizza.

"Wait, how long have we been here?" Billy asked Alyssa.

"About ten minutes, give or take."

"Wow, it feels like we just got here." Cooper was disconcerted.

"Grayson said that would likely happen," said Alyssa. "Normally it's just the first time – you should be okay when we do it again."

"Well aren't you a wealth of information?"

"It's because I ask questions, *William*."

"I.. I think I'll pass on next time," Cooper said, falling onto his back.

Billy took up next to him, plopping down on the grass. "So where are we?"

"Cypremort Point State Park. It's been turned into a refugee camp of sorts, along with triage."

Cooper listened for a moment to the sounds of frogs and crickets. It felt similar to the Greenway back home but the humidity was something else. He felt drenched in sweat and…

Oh geez. I hope I didn't go to the bathroom during the trip, he thought, unwilling to check.

Billy was looking around, noticing ships in the Bay, clusters of trees near the shoreline, and other random structures. "How did we not end up skewered on any number of those objects?"

"Huh, I didn't ask Grayson that question," Alyssa said, embarrassed she'd missed something Billy was cognizant enough to ask about. "I'm sure there's a reason."

"I'm sure," Billy said with a brisk smile. *Yes, I one-upped her!* the smile said.

It wasn't until Cooper and Billy stood up and joined Alyssa at the edge of camp that they realized the extent of the devastation around them. The dreary light at one o'clock in the morning did little to hide the sad and frightened faces of the victims, and nothing to hide the sounds of grief and agony coming from all around. As the three of them stood there looking in, it dawned on them just how far they were from home.

"Should we go in?" Cooper asked.

Alyssa nodded, spotting several injured wolves that looked like they could use some help, or at least someone to talk to.

"Billy, Cooper and I are going to head to that tent over there by the closest cabin."

"Okay," he mumbled, still gawking into the camp. "I'll join you in a few."

"Alright," said Alyssa, and with a gentle, two-fingered rub of Billy's elbow, she started toward the tent with Cooper.

***

Billy watched the two head into camp before his gaze drifted, then lingered on the carnage. Eyes vast, the scene reminded him of the aftermath of the Shadow Wolves' assault on Goodman, and the moments beforehand when he was forced to run and fight for his life down Center Street…

Once he had hidden well enough, the wolves had passed (later learning they were heading to destroy Grayson Manor), he vigilantly returned home on the corner of Grove Road and Cherry Lane to find the bodies of his parents in the front yard – mutilated…

Pressure built deep and unreachable in Billy's chest, while his heart beat like a runaway train. Everything was growing dark at the corners, tunnel vision spreading until…

An encouraging hand clamped down on his shoulder, causing the darkness to fade and his heart to slow down a little.

"Oh thank you Coop," he said, turning to see an unfamiliar face staring back at him, nose ring and all.

"It's never is easy to see things like this," the man said, smiling gently. "My name is Rikolf by the way, and I think you're part of the group Grayson brought with him to help?"

"I… I agree," Billy said, finding the man's voice charming and his look even more so. "And yes! Um, yes. I came along with Grayson, Cooper, and Alyssa."

"You forgot to tell me *your* name."

"Huh? Oh! William… I mean Billy. Billy Arnett."

Rikolf chuckled. "Well, it's a pleasure to meet you Billy Arnett. Look, I know the scene here is quite overwhelming but Grayson tells me that you're no stranger to such things. There's absolutely no need to fret while you're here." Rikolf's grip on Billy's shoulder grew tighter to drive the point home. "You're safe, and with family now."

"Th-thank you," Billy stammered as Rikolf let go.

"Come on then," Rikolf said, "Let's go find Grayson again. I need to have a few more words with him about what's going on."

Rikolf led the way into camp, Billy strategically trailing to watch him walk out in front. He couldn't help but wonder why the wolf (*this really attractive wolf*) was being so kind to him. As Billy pondered, he suddenly remembered the name Rikolf from a brief mention back in Goodman and that – WOAH! – he was the Alpha of the Vermilion Bay Wolves!

Yeah, Billy, don't get too caught up on the niceties! That's exactly what they are, because a wolf like Rikolf would never have time for one like you beyond those simple, required niceties…

2

Billy kept behind Rikolf for a majority of the way along Beach Lane, though his attention was fixed on several triage tents that were filled with injured men, women, and children. Billy couldn't look at them for too long before getting a stifling, sad cramp in his stomach. They also passed by Cooper and Alyssa, who were trying to comfort an older woman. Billy wondered what happened to her to cause that much agony in her wrinkled face, but he suspected he knew exactly what it was. The only question was if it were husband, child, or grandchild.

"Horrific isn't it?" Rikolf asked.

"Yeah," Billy replied flatly. "I've seen this kind of thing twice this month and it's really something I'd never care to see again."

"Me and you both, Billy. I fear that we may yet see this again given the troubles with the Bear King from the Tensas River Basin. I gather you're familiar with the situation?"

Billy told him what he'd learned by means of Cooper, Grayson, and Theryn the avian shifter, Rikolf satisfied that Billy knew the extent and severity of what was happening.

"I have to say, given what you've already been through, for you to be here voluntarily speaks volumes about your character, Billy. Don't change… for there are far greater men of history that have done far less than you have just by being here."

Billy didn't know what to say. He agreed, yet didn't *want* to agree for fear of sounding conceited.

Rikolf could see the debate right there in Billy's darting eyes. "Relax! Remember no worries here."

"I know, it's just difficult to process with everything that's happened and… my own changes."

Thanks to Grayson, Rikolf knew of those changes and told Grayson during the brief chat that he was astonished Billy had managed to survive. Rikolf didn't tell Billy then – it wasn't the right time – but Grayson had told Rikolf that there was far more to Billy than met the eye, and that true courage if ever such a thing existed flowed through his veins.

"Maybe we can talk more about it when things settle down?"

"I'd like that a lot."

"Me too," Rikolf said as Grayson caught up with them.

"Ah, good! I see you two have met," Grayson said happily, he looked to Billy and winked.

Billy didn't know what was going on, but for a moment he excused himself. "Can I get you two anything? I don't want to eavesdrop on your conversation."

"You're more than welcome to stick around," Grayson requested.

"Please do," confirmed Rikolf, "though if you're hard-pressed to do something how about a couple of pieces of jerky from that rack over there?"

Billy smiled and promptly went off toward the stands as Grayson and Rikolf resumed discussions about both past and current events. He snatched three pieces of jerky, attempted to give the person watching over it some money and was told to take it. Munching on his piece when he returned, he handed the other two pieces to Grayson and Rikolf.

"Again, I'm so sorry to hear of Liam," said Rikolf solemnly, taking the dried venison from Billy. "I can't believe the things that happened down in that dreaded Vault. I know Lance was not in anyone's good graces by the end, but I do extend my sympathies to you for the loss of your brother too, my dearest friend."

Grayson looked around, remembering there was a time when Lance was good. "At least I still have a brother-in-law that has character. It would seem that destruction is fast becoming an unwelcome visitor for the both of us. Our last talk was brief, but is there *anyone* left?"

"Very few," Rikolf muttered. "Oh so few, in fact. Those who are left are mainly subordinates, and a few loners that came to aid us from the New Orleans area. But my Beta's body has yet to be discovered, and any Omegas that were here are dead by betrayal."

"So, no one in your the direct line, other than yourself of course?"

"No."

Grayson sighed, and Billy realized that Rikolf was in a similar situation as both he and Grayson. Alone, in the sense of having no direct family to call upon.

Perhaps he could somehow sense your loss and that's why he's been so nice to you? Billy thought. *Wolves can do that right? Smell weird things and feelings?*

"Don't get too caught up in the niceties, Billy," he whispered to himself, but not low enough to be unheard.

"What was that?" asked Grayson.

"Huh? Oh, I was just, um, thinking about how it's ironic the three of us are standing here in a similar situation – without direct family – yet working together toward a common goal to help a lot of others. Makes me feel good."

Grayson shot a proud glance Rikolf's way. "Told you, didn't I?"

"Told him what?" Billy asked inquisitively.

Before Grayson could answer, another wolf approached, still shifted.

"We are still searching for Badric's body, my Alpha. Unless he was somehow thrown into the Bay, we will find him."

Rikolf bowed as the messenger departed. "I hope he turns up, for the remaining wolves are blaming the bears directly and want action. I need to give them something and soon, else it'll be chaos."

"You do realize there is more going on here than some random attacks by a mad bear king?" Grayson urged Rikolf to see beyond Lobjörn.

Rikolf nodded, but said, "Regardless of the demons I know Lobjörn will try to attack again. Mad or not, he's definitely an immediate threat, and one we will need to address far sooner than the Noctis."

Chapter 15

BADRIC'S BETRAYAL

Friday April 12, 2013

1

On a jutting cypress peninsula was a large stump-like throne, surrounded on three sides by the waters of Big Lake. Overhead, great sheets of Spanish moss hung between the treetops, casting an unsettling green light on the surroundings, while thin strands of mist weaved through the shrubbery like a giant, gossamer web.

Badric, the Vermilion Bay Beta, was indeed suitably rattled as he emerged from the trees in his human form, the infamous Tensas Throne coming into view.

"Hello?" he called feebly into the low morning light, hoping there would be no answer.

No answer came (for which he was thankful), the tranquil sounds of insects and wind-blown leaves amounting to a sufficient response.

"Hello?" he repeated for good measure, and when no answer came for the second time, he was truly relieved.

Turning to leave, Badric let out a long sigh, which became a smothered grunt as he hit something hard and immovable. Recovering, his view focused on a vast patch of dark, shabby fur, which rose many feet above his head. Glancing that direction, Badric saw Lobjörn's insipid green eyes staring down, and through him.

"Going somewhere so soon?" the mighty bear growled, causing Badric to take a step back, then another.

"No… no… of course not"

"Then come, let us talk." Lobjörn's beastly weight dropped on all fours, lumbering toward his throne.

Badric gave one last, worried glance over his shoulder. Looking to the forest, he considered running. That is, until he heard distant groans and growls coming from *somewhere* out there in the mist, and promptly reconsidered.

"I just wanted to say, Wolf Beta, that I appreciate the information you provided on The Gathering."

Badric hurried to catch up to the Bear King. "Not as much as I appreciate our bargain," he replied nervously, nearly forgetting to add, "Your Eminence."

Unbeknownst to all but the two standing in the throne room that early morning, Badric had struck a selfish and shortsighted deal with Lobjörn in an attempt to gain power for himself. The Beta would assume control of Vermilion Bay and other lands beyond after the removal of Rikolf as Alpha, in knowing that he and all others would be under Lobjörn's ultimate dominion.

The Bear King reached the throne and stood, stretching tall. He then lowered himself onto the seat, filling it with his monstrous bulk. The wood crackled beneath.

Badric approached cautiously; despite the pleasantries the air was still murky and thick with unease.

"About the bargain," Lobjörn said surreptitiously. "Is there anything… *important* you need to tell me?"

Badric's heart was seized in a vise. *How does he already know?*

"Well?" The single word carried a paragraph's worth of impatience.

Badric's throat became dry, moisture fleeing. Licking his lips did nothing but scrape his tongue, which made his next words all the more difficult to say. "Rikolf and the other shifter Warryn are still alive. They managed to get aid from…"

Lobjörn rose from the throne, looming like a tower. With speed that should not have been possible for something his size, Lobjörn appeared next to the wolf in a flash, one of his massive clawed paws engulfing the entirety of his chest.

"Tell me, why should I not kill you, and every inept red wolf I see from now until the end of time?"

Sweating profusely, Badric's words were fragmented. "B-because, Your Eminence, I… I know that G-Grayson is also t-there."

Lobjörn closed his paw, and Badric grunted as his ribs were pressed against his lungs. His feet left the ground and then, as the pain ramped up so high the wolf felt like he would erupt, it suddenly stopped.

"This is grand news," said Lobjörn optimistically, dropping the wretched wolf to the soil. "All three of them are still there?"

"Yes." Badric drew short breaths, clutching at his chest. He spoke shortly between them. "They've relocated to Cypremort State Park. It's where we go in emergency situations."

"Ah, yes," Lobjörn snickered. "Shifter pride in holding their ground, even if that ground is unstable. Just like Rikolf to do something so bravely stupid."

Badric stood up, swaying, and stepped closer to Lobjörn to schmooze. "I... I would be more than happy to show you the –" Badric's words were cut abruptly mid-sentence, just as his throat was sliced.

Lobjörn had used a single claw to do the deed, having swung it outward and upward. There it remained, buried in the wolf's lower jaw. "It's okay, Wolf Beta, I think I'll be able to do this myself."

Then, before Badric could understand, never mind accept what had happened (beyond the searing pain spreading through his body), life left him, never to return. He had died without his pack, and without a legacy, just as he deserved.

Chapter 16

BILLY'S BOND

Saturday April 13, 2013

1

"Come on, it should be quiet up here…"

The sky was lightening slowly as two figures made their way through the camp at Cypremort State Park, heading toward the northernmost cabin. The taller of the two reached the log building first, prowling around the edges to check that there was nobody else around. A quick thumbs up indicated that it was clear, and the two disappeared around the corner.

"Just like I thought," said Rikolf enthusiastically, grabbing Billy's hand and tugging him closer. "Nobody's around at the moment."

Billy crashed awkwardly into his chest, and after steadying themselves, the two loitered there in a wordless intimacy, their faces close but not touching, their noses drawing in appealing scents that stirred the mind and more. Other urges were certainly there, but would have to wait for when there was more time.

It had only been a few days since Billy had arrived in Vermilion Bay and met Rikolf (a part of him suspecting that wink of Grayson's played a large part in it). Despite or perhaps because of the impending doom that was Lobjörn and the demons, Billy found his thoughts often returning to the man – and wolf – that he could relate to so well, and even though he had told himself to ignore the niceties, they were coming at him with such a quickness that deflecting all of them was impossible.

"I'm glad we're finally alone," Billy said. "I was starting to think we'd never get a chance to…"

"Get to know each other a little more?"

Billy nodded. "I mean, don't get me wrong, all the meetings have been great but, and this may sound incredibly strange, it's been like I've been *needing* to see you privately."

"Nah, that sounds incredibly lovey-dovey," Rikolf replied, lightly laughing with a hint of a crooked smirk, "but you want to know the sad part? I feel the same way, and trust me when I say I haven't for a very long time."

There was a pause, the silence only broken by the sounds of lapping water on the shore.

Billy looked out toward the bayou, the first hints of sunrise spreading across the view. He lifted his gazed toward Rikolf. "I... I don't want to get my hopes up for anything," Billy said dejectedly.

"Then don't," said Rikolf plainly, though when his fingers interlocked with Billy's and their hands arrived at chest level, the sentiment was different.

"These emotions are so complicated," Billy sputtered, and to his surprise Rikolf's lips pressed on his forehead. They remained there for a few long seconds before Rikolf pulled back.

"That they definitely are." The crooked smirk was back, more pronounced. "But in all seriousness, let's just see where things go... no hopes for anything, just riding the wave."

Billy was unsure how to do that; he'd always been one for setting goals, no matter how mundane (like working at Rabun Paving after graduation). Yet Rikolf had the ability to change Billy's mind with a look, and he was doing that look right then.

"Okay," Billy said anxiously, and eagerly.

New territory yet again! Yippie Skippy!

"So in that vein," Rikolf said, using his hands to grab Billy's shoulders and rub them. "I have patrol tonight – mainly covering the outer banks of the Bay, checking for nasties and that sort of thing. I can always have you go with me instead of one of the other subordinates…"

Rikolf managed to steal away Billy's breath.

"If you'd like to of course," Rikolf added.

Billy found himself grabbing hold of the belt loops in Rikolf's scraggly jeans. As Billy pulled him closer and they touched, he could feel that they both had the same idea about that night; the same *hope* that they'd agreed not to…

But there's nothing wrong with anticipation, Billy thought, especially if they were both happy for it.

"How can I say no to that?" Billy answered, and leaning in he kissed Rikolf, unable to wait until that night when they could be alone, together.

2

Night finally came after an eternally long day filled with planning, meetings, and waiting. Somewhere off the soggy shores of Vermilion Bay, heavy paws thumped and splashed their way across the marshy soil, the noise stirring the soupy air.

All was good, and Billy Arnett – with the wind rushing across his muzzle and mud squelching between his claws – let out a beastly howl. It was joined by another from a large, shaggy wolf with reddish- brown hair that was running, or rather racing, beside him.

"Come on slow poke!" Rikolf hounded, and in a delirious fit of laughter he darted ahead of Billy like a bolt fired from a crossbow.

"Oh! You think you've got me?" Billy shouted, and his stride increased with great leaps and bounds.

Both creatures dashed across the land, their feet kicking up silt and sludge, the dark water trying its best to hang on their fur in clumps.

"First one to those trees over there wins!" Rikolf charged.

"You would pick those since they're closer to you!" Billy grunted. "Only way you'd win!"

The chosen finish line was a collection of misshapen trees on a round hill, resembling an island of sorts rising out from the swampy surroundings.

Billy was focused on the destination, bound and determined to show Rikolf who was boss. Then, something else drew his attention away. It was fleeting and bizarre, lingering just out of full view in the corner of his eye. Billy slowed to see if he could make it out any better.

"Hey Billy!" Rikolf called. "What're you up to?" The gap between the two grew with each passing second.

Billy looked around. Whatever it was had gone. Unable to see what he thought he saw anymore, he resumed the run. He could see Rikolf's eyes bulge as he realized how fast Billy was approaching, and Billy bet that if Rikolf didn't know the massive creature was friendly, he would have been terrified.

I know because I terrify myself at times, Billy thought. *A lot these days…*

Rikolf turned his head and rushed at full speed for the trees.

Billy's legs were aching, but he continued forward as hard and fast as he could.

The gap was closing.

The trees were getting closer.

And then, suddenly both Rikolf and Billy tumbled, their feet stopped by a sunken log.

Rikolf spun through the air and was first to careen into the muck, Billy a close second, crashing on top of him with a resounding *plop*. After a few seconds, the two emerged from the gurgling mess, plastered.

"I guess it was a tie," Billy huffed, only his red eyes and mouth free of mud. That is, until a huge glob leeched its way into his mouth.

"If you say so," Rikolf said offhandedly, watching Billy try to spit the mud out, his long tongue flapping and all. "Though technically I was the first to face plant."

"You can have the title then!" Billy laughed, a strange sound like a lion mixed with a gorilla. Rikolf joined him, right before splashing a tidal wave's worth of sludge at Billy.

Billy retaliated in turn, excavating two huge paw-sized globs of filth. Catapulting them, the muddy artillery flew through the air and smacked Rikolf right back down into the murk. He emerged a few moments later and the two resumed their earlier, beastly laughter.

"Haha! Let's get cleaned off and rest a minute," Rikolf suggested, moving out into deeper water.

"Don't we have to finish the patrol?" Billy asked, following.

"It can wait for a few minutes," Rikolf responded, and after the two washed themselves, Rikolf led Billy toward the trees and laid down on the mossy hillside.

"Now I see why you picked this place," Billy said as he laid beside him, the two brutes looking out at the peaceful panorama.

"Exactly," Rikolf replied, observing Billy. "What slowed you down, by the way? You were definitely going to win until then."

"I'm not sure what I saw," Billy said sheepishly. "It was like, and don't think I'm crazy, but I swear I saw a stag being *escorted* by a couple of alligators or crocodiles – I don't know the difference – but that can't be right at all, can it?"

"You sound like Elric." Rikolf threw his head back, exhaling. "I'm going to miss him and his unique brand of optimism."

"Was he…?"

"Yeah, he was an Omega, one of those killed in the rebel attack. Billy, I don't think you're crazy at all, but I do think the old stories from this area are quite haunting and, for want of a better word, magical. Those tales tend to imbue everything – the cities, the trees, the bayous, Elric – with an essence that helps this place endure. It's also part of what makes those who live here endure."

Billy's eyes were bright. "So, what I saw was something from those old stories?"

"What you probably saw was just a deer about to be those gator's dinner."

"If you say so," Billy said lowly, unable to understand how a legendary monster like a werewolf could doubt the existence of something else that was (as Rikolf said, for want of a better word) magical.

3

Billy took a moment to shift into his human form, still nestled against Rikolf's fur. It felt good against his naked skin, if not a little rough.

"Now that things have settled enough for us to have that promised chat, tell me some about your past," Rikolf requested.

Billy considered the time and their responsibility to finish the patrol, but he wasn't about to argue with an Alpha about it. So, he ended up telling Rikolf about his life in Goodman – from his early years, to the encounter with Derek Wilder on Halloween 2005 and meeting Cooper Bennett, to his developing feelings for Cooper since that day and the jealousy he encountered upon seeing him and Alyssa together.

"I can definitely relate to that," Rikolf said, in more ways than one. "Boundaries, friendships, duty, it's all a difficult balance to maintain a status quo that could easily tip in any direction."

"And more often than not that direction isn't a good one, either," Billy added, telling Rikolf about their dealings with the Mannings, Lance Goddard and the losses he dealt, and his own destiny in the jaws of the Gray Mother.

"All that happening to you in such a short time," Rikolf mumbled. "I don't know if I could have handled it. You see, most of my hurdles have come in waves, but over a far longer timeframe." Rikolf paused, spending a moment admiring Billy's naked body against him before continuing.

"I'd met a man years ago from a nearby town called Baldwin. His name was Jonathan Sparks – an ironic name now that I think about it, since he'd sparked so many new aspects of my life and showed me avenues I knew nothing about but had so much potential. I found myself smitten with him and his freedom, but my role as the Beta of Vermilion Bay would never lend itself to going down any of those new avenues with him. The right to a mate is reserved for Alphas only, as you know, and even then the fact that it was a human I was in love with, and a human male at that, well that would have made matters a hundred times worse.

"Despite that, our love somehow managed to endure and we took to seeing each other in secret. I took the rather silly name of Rick Oft, along with the identity of a construction worker from Baton Rouge. I figured being from the capital, and it being in a different parish altogether, would have made it more difficult for Jonathan to find out the truth about me."

"Couldn't he have just looked you up on the internet?" Billy asked. "Not that I stalk many… I mean *any*body like that."

"Well, times were different back then"

"'Back then'?" Billy questioned. "How long ago was that?"

"Some, well, a long time ago."

Billy grumbled something incoherent, and Rikolf smiled.

"You mentioned being in a different 'parish'. Are the wolves down here more religious or something?"

"Not sure what the wolves all around the world are like," Rikolf stated, "but parishes here are like counties elsewhere."

Billy's expression was like a light bulb being turned on. "So, Rabun County at home would be Rabun Parish here? How weird."

Rikolf nodded, adding, "It's mainly due to the state's Roman Catholic history. The borders of the counties match up with the old parish lines, roughly, and so the term's stuck around ever since."

"Interesting," Billy said, "and still weird."

Rikolf continued his story, telling Billy that the two men saw each other for a time, their hidden romance ending tragically when a careless night of drinking forced their relationship into the light.

"Some of the more rebellious members of the pack took to beating Jonathan within an inch of his life. The motive was mainly if not entirely racist – humans being what they are and certain, underlying feelings in some wolves needing to get out."

Billy's jaw dropped as Rikolf told him what happened next.

"I was enraged, and I attacked, killing two of the wolves from my own pack. The third was spared only when my Father interjected. Then, surprisingly, he did the deed himself, killing the last wolf and therefore removing all witnesses. He ordered me to never speak of the incident or my feelings for humans again, else suffer the same fate. We blamed the killings on rowdy rednecks, and nobody was ever the wiser."

Billy gulped harshly, wondering why Rikolf was trusting him enough with this information. He also wondered if his own parents would have been so ashamed. He liked to think they wouldn't be, but he'd never know for sure now.

Rikolf adjusted himself, Billy settling further into his fur. "Now, today, things are different," Rikolf said. "With everything and everyone gone, I feel both a terrible sadness yet relief. Lots and lots of relief. After such an uphill battle with my life, I'm finally free to pursue the things that make me happy, for the sole reason that it pleases me. Something tells me that you, too, have that opportunity Billy Arnett."

Billy didn't answer that right away, instead looking off to the dark lands around them. "I do feel that freedom," he said wistfully, "but would be lying if I didn't say I was scared."

"Of being alone?"

"Yeah. Being alone and messing up with nobody there to catch me if I fall."

"That's how we grow," Rikolf stated.

"And how we get hurt," Billy responded.

"They're one and the same thing, my friend. That pain we feel leads to lessons, which, in turn, lead to improvements."

Billy nodded subtly. "But Coop…"

"Cooper will be fine." Rikolf said sternly. "He has his new mate, Alyssa, and a new life to live among his own people."

Billy was quiet again. The look on his face saying he thought he *was* one of "Cooper's people".

"You do too," Rikolf continued.

"I do what?"

"Have a new life to live. That is, if you want it."

Billy's heart started to beat faster, but strangely the anger that had accompanied it since the Change was not there. Instead, he felt at ease. Looking up at the sky – spangled with a swath of milky stars – Rikolf's coarse hair twirled between Billy's fingers.

"I would like that very much. I… I could definitely get used to this," Billy muttered, then smiled as the Vermilion wolf replied…

"I already have."

Rikolf shifted into human form, and Billy could feel his hair pull away, replaced by smooth skin and large, taunt arms that wrapped themselves around him.

Rikolf bent over, his lips gently touching the top of Billy's head. He took a long breath. "You smell good."

Billy chuckled, reaching up to flick that nose ring of Rikolf's. "You smell awful. Like you've been swimming in swamp muck."

"You should get used to it in time."

"Ironically," Billy said, smirking, "I already have…"

It was then that their eyes met in the twilight, and Billy felt a flutter of excitement start in his stomach, move toward his chest, and back again.

"What's the matter?" Rikolf asked, gently sliding himself on top of Billy, whose back he helped rest on the soft moss.

"Nothing," Billy said with a content smile accompanying the slightest giggle. "At last… nothing at all."

He then closed his eyes, feeling soft lips press against his own, along with every naked inch of Rikolf's muscular body.

Billy's hands roamed while they kissed, following the hills and valleys of Rikolf's shoulders and back, claws forming when Rikolf beard started brushing against Billy's neck, then digging into his skin when Rikolf's hips began to grind.

Rikolf started to kiss Billy's collar area upon feeling the pleasant scratching at his back, his nose trapped in a well of intoxicating scents and tastes, while his hands became entangled in long strands of dark, messy hair.

Soon their lips worked their way to each other again. Their smooth bodies spoke to wanting more, Billy welcoming Rikolf as they continued to make love beneath the waxing crescent moon.

It was, in short, like a dream. Yet, the warm reality of it all was all this had happened in less than a month – life having a way of directing unsuspecting feet on paths they didn't even know they were walking. From the loss of his parents during that horrific Shadow Wolf attack, to entering a catacomb-like Vault beneath a small town – his *hometown* – only to be bitten by the first werewolf that ever walked the Earth and become a shifter (the most rare).

Beyond that, and thanks to it, he was able to grow strengthened bonds of friendship and family with Cooper, Alyssa, Grayson and now, right up to where he was that Saturday night hundreds of miles from home in swampy Louisiana, Rikolf – a ring-nosed Alpha with all the allure and charm he'd been missing, and much needing, in his life.

If someone had asked Billy Arnett just one month ago if he would have imagined any of that happening, he would have said, "No way, but let me know what obscure television shows and movies you're watching for inspiration, because I've definitely been missing out!"

Chapter 17

FRIENDLY CONCERNS

1

"Do you think the extra bears Svarbjörn's sent will be enough if the other Bear King attacks?"

Alyssa was walking down a dark LA-339, the shops at Vermilion Bay forty minutes to her back, the state park about twenty minutes ahead, and Cooper immediately at her side. They were hiking back with unofficial "supplies" from the few shops that were there – mainly sweets and snacks – but the time away from the carnage was definitely the more refreshing resource.

"I'm sure they'll be enough for him", Cooper answered positively, "especially since we're expecting him this time; the element of surprise he had with the rebel wolves is gone. Now, if the demons come marching in with him or after, then we may have some trouble on our hands."

Alyssa shook her head in disbelief, thinking about all the children she'd seen hurt or worse. "I can't imagine what kind of person… *monster* could do that to defenseless children."

"The same kind that can do it to defenseless animals. The world is full of monsters, baby, and they come in many forms – most not legendary in the least."

"Do you think we'll encounter something like that with the Shadow Wolves? That kind of betrayal?"

"We can almost count on it," replied Cooper glumly. "Rodric wasn't about to let me take over as Shadow Alpha without a fight, and I'm sure there are others who feel the same but are keeping their feelings on the down low."

Alyssa didn't like that feeling of constantly having to watch your back. In school, she had "friends" that could double as enemies at the same time they were smiling at you, she was glad to see the backside of them when her life deepened too much for shallow people to survive. Now, she was stepping into an existence where her vigilance would be tested daily. There was just no escaping that sort of thing, it seemed.

What doesn't kill you makes you stronger, right? she thought woefully. "It's all just, wow, so much to take in. I mean we were just thinking about college, what, a couple of months ago? And just last month thinking about people-watching drunk idiots at the Goodman edition of Saint Patrick's Day. I'm sure someone would have made the *Courier*'s front page with their antics."

"Something tells me old man Kensington still wouldn't be happy with those headlines."

The two laughed brightly.

"Yeah, you're right," Alyssa said, still giggling.

"Speaking of people-watching," Cooper added as the laughter died, "have you noticed how well Billy and that Alpha have been getting along?"

"'That Alpha'? You mean Rikolf?"

"Yeah, him," Cooper said tersely.

"I have…" Alyssa continued carefully, fully aware that Cooper's tone seemed less than enthusiastic about the two of them hanging out. "Do you have a problem with Rikolf?"

"No," Cooper replied shortly. "Why would I? Billy's entitled to live his own life and do as he pleases."

Growing tired of Cooper's quick temper and considering his apparent flip-flopping between opinions like a fish out of water, Alyssa didn't answer.. Instead, she took to listening to the *pitter patter* of their soles as they walked back to camp. Baffled, she glanced to Cooper, seeing an expression that plainly said he was in no mood to talk. Wondering what was going on in that confused mind of his now, she sighed and looked out across the swamplands, missing the mountains of home…

2

About half an hour later, Cooper and Alyssa returned to their pagoda tent. Originally used for special occasions such as weddings at the park, the much larger original units had been divided, their pieces repurposed into makeshift accommodations, medical units, and a cafeteria.

Alyssa pulled back the rather stiff white canvas and entered the rectangular space. There were arched windows built in along the far wall, allowing some of the limited outside light through. A simple wooden table had been set up in the middle of the room. A couple of lanterns were on its top, their warm light illuminating four chairs pushed underneath, while the same number of sleeping bags were scattered along the edges.

She fussily dropped off her bags at the table, then pulled out one of the chairs and fell into it. Using the backrest to prop up her arms, she rested her chin, and closed her eyes.

Cooper did the same, though he just dropped his with a notable *thud*, which caused Alyssa's eyelids to shoot open again.

"What the hell is wrong with you?" she asked, alongside a disapproving stare.

"Nothing," he pouted in an attempt to brush it off. He might as well have stomped his foot or stuck his tongue out for how bratty he looked.

"Oh come on, I'm not that stupid." She rolled her eyes. You even helped me get rid of the blonde hair to underscore that fact."

Cooper looked at her and tried to bottle a laugh, knowing full well that she wasn't stupid and that he was being a child. He pulled out the chair opposite her and crashed into it himself. Bending over, he pressed his face deep into his palms. "I'm not sure what's wrong with me," Cooper said. "I think I'm just being overprotective of him after the argument we had on Wolf's Ridge."

"Probably, because we both know you care about him a lot. I do too."

"He's like a brother to me," Cooper replied.

"Yes, and more..." Alyssa added. "Again, I'm not stupid Cooper."

Cooper groaned, then let out a long, pensive sigh. *Oh great,* the gestures said.

"Look, don't think that I'm not concerned about Billy," said Alyssa, "it's just I know that he has to live his own life, and whatever he decides is best for him you and me should support that. It's his choice."

"Even if that choice has him leaping into a volcano?"

"Rikolf is *not* a volcano!"

"Geez!" Cooper moaned, throwing himself into the back of the chair. It tipped, nearly to the point of falling over. While Cooper was pleased to see Billy happy at last, he had to ask Alyssa, "Doesn't it seem to be going awfully fast to you?"

"Yes," Alyssa replied succinctly, and Cooper's face lit up that she agreed.

"And no," she also said succinctly, Cooper's face falling flatter than ten-day-old soda.

"I mean, Coop, we got together pretty damn fast if you think about it, and we seem fine."

"If you say so…" Cooper shrugged, and Alyssa didn't look amused. "But we knew each other for years," Cooper added.

"We knew *of* each other. I seem to recall a boy with a *Q-tip* for a head and zero muscles asking me to prom."

Cooper groaned loudly, followed by a weak laugh. "Liam didn't seem to want that happening anytime soon, either, did he?"

"No," Alyssa said softly, "he didn't. I think, honestly Cooper, you're not ready to say goodbye to Billy, but you know as well as I do that his time to leave is inevitably coming."

Cooper was silent, but bobbed his head. A short time later, he broke the silence with a question. "Speaking of prom, I still owe that to you, don't I?"

"I don't think we're going to find anything like that anywhere out here." Alyssa was puzzled, her snicker nervous.

Cooper stood up from his chair, extending a hand. "Well, how about a dance then?"

"Seriously?" Alyssa asked, and Cooper answered by reaching into his pocket.

"Yes, seriously," he said to her while he toyed with his phone. A moment later, through a struggling signal, Asher Lane started singing about *New Days*. "Give me a chance to say 'sorry' for being an absolute dick tonight. Come on, Miss Noble, may I have this dance?"

Alyssa's hand fell into his, and Cooper lifted her out of the chair before pulling her toward him. Grabbing her waist, he led her outside with gentle twirls where they spent time together in an awkward yet romantic dance beneath a starlit sky.

Chapter 18

VERMILION BAY RUNS RED (II)

Sunday April 14, 2013

1

Well rested, Cooper and Alyssa were sitting under the cafeteria tent for breakfast. There were three long picnic tables beneath the fluttering canopy; the duo sat along the middle one. At one end of the structure was a set of chafing dishes on neat, white tables, their little cans of fuel burning away to heat the buffet. The other end housed a hurriedly erected outdoor kitchen, where a manic, tall cook was busy arguing with the much calmer (and much shorter) chef from the seafood market.

"Can you make out what they're saying?" Alyssa prodded with a whisper for Cooper to listen.

"No," he replied after trying again, seeing their lips moving but hearing the teacher's voice from *Charlie Brown.* "They're speaking awfully fast in a foreign language. I think it's French."

Cooper resumed stabbing his food with a fork while the background melody of French insults continued to play. Something about the bacon and eggs tasted odd. Maybe the fact he now knew boar and bird shifters existed was the culprit.

Alyssa had just started on her bowl of milky oatmeal when Billy plopped down right beside her with a gigantic smile on his face. "Well! Look at you all bright-eyed and bushy-tailed this morning!" she observed, followed by a piping spoonful of those oats topped with honey and almonds.

One guess as to what you got into last night, Cooper thought, muttering the same thing aloud but incoherently.

"What was that Coop?" asked Billy casually, still beaming.

"Oh," Cooper replied, catching Alyssa giving him that same *stop being bratty* look that he'd gotten the night before. "You seem to have had a good night. Who, I mean what, did you end up getting in to?"

Alyssa grumbled as she took another bite, this time slurping to underscore her displeasure.

"Rikolf," Billy said serenely. "He took me out on patrol last night. We went around the north side of the Bay. Gosh it was great."

"Did you see anything interesting?" Alyssa asked, casting a look to Cooper that said *don't you even think about it!*

"You're going to think I'm nuts, but I thought I saw a stag being escorted by some alligators! Strangest thing I'd ever seen – well, at least since earlier in the week when we found out about all these other kinds of shifters."

"That definitely sounds out of the ordinary," Alyssa agreed. "What'd Rikolf have to say about it?"

"He said I was crazy."

"Well, he got that right," Alyssa said, laughing along with Billy.

Cooper ended up stabbing the middle of his over-easy egg. The yolk ran out and over the plate; it looked just like his mood felt.

"This place is just surreal," Billy continued, still cheerful. "The stories, the people, the food, *everything* about it seems just like home but... deeper. I don't know if that makes much sense."

"It does actually," Alyssa said, looking toward Cooper. "It sounds like you've found a place that reminds you of home."

"I guess so," Billy said cheerily. "I mean, I just got here, so it'd take some time to see... but I can see it being home – in some ways at least."

This time Cooper felt Billy's eyes on him, and he knew what those last few words meant.

"Heck, Alyssa's asking all the questions this morning!" Billy said. "Are you feeling alright, buddy?"

Alyssa cringed and Billy noticed. "Sorry, hot spoonful!" she said, still watching Cooper.

"Yeah I have a question for you, did you guys do it?"

"Cooper!" Alyssa shouted, even getting the attention of the arguing cooks.

"What? I just wanted to know," Cooper replied.

"Know *what*, exactly?" Billy asked, surprisingly self-assured. "If he's *bigger* than you?"

Cooper scoffed. Alyssa choked.

"Huge," Billy said. "Monstrous…"

Alyssa downed some water. Cooper rolled his eyes.

But Billy wasn't done yet. "So yeah. It was big, like as long as my…"

"Oh hello there!" Alyssa cut across Billy, speaking to Rikolf as he joined them.

"How is everyone this morning?" he asked, unaware of the previous conversation. He took a seat beside Billy.

"Good," said Alyssa. "Lovely breakfast."

"Short, apparently," said Cooper smugly.

Alyssa kicked him under the table, causing Cooper to jolt.

"Are you okay?" Rikolf asked, concerned.

"Oh, he's fine," Billy said. "Just a bit of his *Jellitis* flaring up again."

Rikolf laughed, as did Alyssa. Cooper on the other hand did not, shoving the unpleasant bacon in his mouth. He wasn't even chewing. Once the laughter faded Rikolf was left smiling at Billy. He was holding out a fist.

"Here. This is for you."

Billy looked at him curiously and opened his hand. A small, pewter cross dropped into it, inscribed with an abbreviated version of Acts 20:24.

"However, I consider my life worth nothing to me; my only aim is to finish the race and complete the task the Lord Jesus has given me," Billy recited.

Rikolf placed one of his hands over Billy's and told him that, "This was Jonathan's, the man I told you about last night, and now, Billy, it's yours."

Alyssa was near tears, her cheeks lifted by a smile and rosy red.

Wide-eyed Billy attached it to the chain that held his white ring, and Cooper – feeling an absolute fool – looked down toward his black one.

"I am glad you're here, Shadow Alpha," said Rikolf.

Surprised to hear such a thing, Cooper looked up and saw Rikolf staring at him. "Why is that?"

Rikolf smiled. "Beyond the physical support you've provided as a true Alpha, just bringing this feeling of family around. It's been a long time since I've felt this, and I am incredibly happy that –"

Suddenly, harsh horns were blowing, filling the camp with the knowledge that the perimeter had been breached by foes.

Rikolf assumed control quickly. He stood, and looking toward the sunrise urgently said, "The Bear King is here!"

2

Lobjörn was approaching Cypremort State Park from the east, his forces moving along LA-319, his numbers spreading into the marshy lands to its north.

The Alphas of Vermilion Bay, the White Wolves, and the Shadow Wolves held a line on the eastern edge of the camp. Also gathered were a handful of Svarbjörn's Defenders of the Realm, the vestiges of fight-capable Vermilion subordinates, and lone wolves from neighboring territories. Billy was also there, Alyssa too. A small canal normally used for canoes and fishing acted as a buffer to control access to the area, which was only reachable by land via a narrow land-bridge on the south side. This arrangement would not hold off the Tensas forces for long, but it could be used to their advantage, at least until reinforcements from the Aves arrived.

"I knew I should have walled this place in," Rikolf lamented as a warm breeze swept through his hair.

Cooper watched as the Alpha looked over his rag-tag force of shifters. He knew he was hoping that it would be enough against Lobjörn's forces; they all did.

"Now is not the time for doubt," Grayson said. "The Bear King has little, and will try to use every ounce of ours against us."

"You are right in your wisdom as always," Rikolf stated.

"Well, I wouldn't go so far as to say *that*," Grayson added, sending a smile Cooper's way.

"There is little time to react!" Rikolf cried. "Subordinates, listen! We need to send the injured men, women, and children west by ship. They have suffered enough at the hands of this cowardly bear. As for the rest of us, we cannot allow Lobjörn to destroy us. This is our home that he is trying to wipe us from, our very history he is trying to erase! Long have the wolves of this region been forced to suffer and move by the will of others. As your Alpha, I say ENOUGH! Now is not the time for fear! Now is the time for Vermilion Bay to say NO MORE!"

The camp erupted into a roar of cheers and shouts. Moments later wolves were rushing into position while others returned west, busying themselves with evacuating the injured and infirm.

"Alyssa," Cooper said, latching onto her shoulders. "I know you came into this life for me but this is the first time that choice will be put to the test. I need you to do what you do best in *this* case, and help those people get to the ships to evacuate. Your level head has saved me several times before, and I need to know that these others might have a better chance with you at their side."

"Okay," she said, voice shaky, "if that's what you feel is best."

"I do…"

Alyssa closed her eyes and nodded, grabbed Cooper's cheeks, and kissed him. Then, turning, she raced back toward the tents. Cooper noticed Grayson was coming up the hill and that he stopped her, handing off some items that Cooper assumed would help the evacuation. On seeing him, Grayson's words from their conversation at the bus station rose out of the silence in his mind, and he understood what he meant completely.

From one Alpha to another: the true test of your resolve hasn't even started yet.

"That was one of the hardest things I've had to do," Cooper admitted, seeing Billy approach his side.

"You did good, buddy," Billy said, placing a hand to Cooper's back as Alyssa disappeared amongst the crowd. "You know I'm here for you. We both are."

Soon after the conflict began – the exact passage of time lost to the chaos of both trauma and stress – Lobjörn had arrived at the eastern side of the camp, lining the far shore of the canal. The forces he'd brought were comprised of shifters still in human form; Cooper assumed they were bears from the Tensas River Basin based on their number and disheveled appearance. Also present were the remaining rebel wolves (already transformed), and a strange contraption near the back of the formation that reminded Cooper of some kind of medieval wagon. It had four large and spindly wheels below a flat platform. A vertical rectangle made of metal rested on that, with horizontal slits near the tops of each side. At that distance, whatever was inside could not be seen.

Far less in number than Cooper expected to see, he didn't let that sway his caution. He knew that Lobjörn's arrogance played a part in this strategy, and that in no way diminished the chances of dying, nor the Bear King's desire to see it done.

"Denizens of Vermilion Bay!" Lobjörn called out with a booming voice betraying the size of his own human form. "At least those of you still able to hear me. Rejoice! For your new ruler has arrived to usher in a dawn of peace and prosperity. Lower your defenses, relinquish yourself to the Tensas River Basin, and find yourselves saved."

"I want access to whatever good wine he's been drinking," Billy whispered to Cooper.

"'Saved'? From what exactly do we need saving from Bear King?" Rikolf shouted across the canal. "The only thing I see that we need to be free of is you!"

Lobjörn smirked wickedly, his voice nothing more than a murmur as he said, "Such shortsightedness in the face of adversity." He then raised it again. "You know there is a greater threat than us looming on the horizon Rikolf!"

"Yes, and my statement still stands Lobjörn! I see only the Bear King before me – the one who destroyed my home and killed my people. I see no demons here, and until I do, they are nothing but rumors!"

"Really? Then let me open your eyes," Lobjörn bellowed, and with a flourish of his hand, several of his troops pushed the bizarre cart forward.

"Oh, this can't be good," said Billy as the wagon advanced to the water's edge.

Then, Lobjörn's men grabbed hold of cranks that were mounted on either side of the cart. Grunting, they rotated them, and with each turn there were loud *clangs* and the sounds of things sliding. After four turns the noises stopped, and all the sides fell away to reveal a cage inside, made of banded iron. Inside that, tied up with simple rope, was a man.

"Who is this?" Rikolf said, unimpressed.

"The very thing you deny is a threat, my canine friend." Lobjörn then stepped toward the cage, his right hand held out and high. "You can learn quite a few things by studying ancient texts, or torturing those they are written about. Isn't that right… Camio?"

Camio, who was broken and battered from the Bear King's hospitality, looked up. His crimson eyes were distant yet evil.

"Regna terrae, cantata Deo, psallite Cernunnos," Lobjörn spoke a Latin phrase unknown to Cooper, and suddenly the man began to convulse. It was an exorcism. *"Regna terrae, cantata Dea psallite Aradia. caeli Deus, Deus terrae…"*

Dropping to his knees, the man shrieked. It was loud, far louder than any human could scream. The sound pierced Cooper's ears, and his hands shot up to do what they could to block out the noise. It made him afraid – a deep fear that resided in the dark recesses of every living being. He couldn't escape the feeling; it was terror incarnate, and it was tremendously frightening even though contained.

Lobjörn was smiling erratically, Cooper thinking he would continue this onslaught for the pleasure it seemed to bring him. To his surprise, the Bear King lowered his hand, and the man's screaming faded into a whimpering sob.

Breathless, Cooper looked around, finding the rest of the allies were like he was; shocked and dismayed by what they had witnessed – or more felt – inside themselves.

"I make this offer a second time; there will not be a third." Lobjörn's countenance was severe. "Relinquish yourself to the Tensas River Basin, and find yourselves saved from this menace."

Rikolf closed his eyes, the wind sweeping across the Bay. For a moment Cooper thought the Alpha was going to agree to the terms, yet hope prevailed (even if it was a fool's hope), and Rikolf opened his eyes once again and said, "NO!"

Lobjörn's triumphant expression turned sour. "Well, I am disappointed, but not surprised Rikolf. I have never liked the Vermilion wolves and their panache for weakness. Your sister Freya had the right idea: to escape to more superior stock with the White Wolves – at least superior in your own mangey minds."

"We are *all* children of the Gray Mother," Rikolf challenged.

"That bloated monstrosity? Ha!"

Angered, the wolves unleashed a thunderous, unified roar.

"At least we can recognize our parent's faults and learn from them," Grayson said, taking a turn to address Lobjörn. "Your forebears were just as hideously inferior as ours, Bear King, as we all stem from the Mother of All Monsters. If you had indeed read those ancient texts you spoke of you'd know this, but it would seem this 'panache of weakness' as you put it has become most pronounced in the Tensas Basin."

Suddenly the bears roared in reply, and Lobjörn joined them, sending his men toward the canal. Many leaped into the water, shifting into beasts while in midair. Another contingent of both wolves and bears made way for the land bridge that was to the south at Beach Lane.

"Everyone!" Rikolf rallied. "It has begun! Stay vigilant! Stay true!"

The Defenders of the Realm took off, thundering toward the land-bridge, and when they arrived they crashed into the Tensas bears with a bulky assault of blood and claws. There were groans of agony, and some of victory, but the main sound was of many breaths escaping bodies for the last time.

The swimming forces crossed the channel, paddling with speed. From afar, Rikolf's forces shot silver-tipped arrows and bolts into wolves and bears alike, felling many but not enough. Blood filled the swirling canal and that red tide reached the western shore. Chaos erupted, and the forces loyal to Rikolf began falling under the pressure of the assault.

Lobjörn strode confidently into the camp by way of Beach Lane, his sharp claws cutting their way through any Vermilion hides that got too close. He thought he'd make it deep within the camp, but didn't make it far. The two Alphas he wanted to see dead more than anyone were waiting on him.

"Ah! So we come to it at last!" Lobjörn said assertively. "I have been looking forward to this!"

"Do you ever stop talking?" Rikolf asked, transforming into his rugged beast form. He growled menacingly, taking a defensive stance once the Change had finished.

Grayson immediately followed suit, the silver-haired man's clothes tearing away before his gleaming white wolf form stood out like a beacon of light among the dark smoke and fires consuming the camp.

"Well aren't you both remarkably pretty?" Lobjörn derided, then looked to each side once he'd spotted Cooper and Billy. The boys were just standing there. "And who are you two lost children?"

"Who are we?" Cooper repeated, eyes sparking with green fire as they both changed into their grisly forms at the same time. He landed with authority, salt and pepper fur blowing in the wind, and as Cooper roared he stepped forward with teeth bared.

"We're your undoing," growled Billy, the dire wolf spreading his arms wide before slamming them into the ground, much to Lobjörn's surprise.

"You're outnumbered, Lobjörn," Rikolf stated, offering the Bear King one last opportunity to stand down. "What you're doing is wrong! Surely you can see reason?"

Lobjörn was quiet at first, surveying the four monsters in front of him with meticulous care. Then, he started to breathe sharply through his nose, chest heaving while his nostrils flared. "No…" Lobjörn said as he transformed himself, the man doubling in size, his voice deepening. "What I am doing is right, and besides, Rikolf, your Beta agreed with me!"

While it was dawning on Rikolf what the Bear King meant by that statement, Lobjörn was already rushing toward him.

"Watch out!" Grayson said, leaping in front of Rikolf only to be swatted away like a fly.

Rikolf retaliated, landing several swipes and two deep, skin-tearing bites on Lobjörn's side. It was then that he noticed the Bear King was wearing something around his neck; a piece of jewelry that had not broken off during his Change. With little time to consider things, Rikolf assumed it was enchanted like his nose ring, but far more insidious.

"He has on some kind of amulet!" Rikolf shouted for the rest to hear, but then a swift blow sent him barreling into the ground. His back was aching from the impact, and Rikolf struggled to get up as Lobjörn advanced toward him.

Cooper was the first of the others to notice it, and something told him he knew what it was. There was a familiarity upon seeing that amulet, yet he knew that he'd never seen it before. As he took a step toward the Bear King, a strange, otherworldly chill rushed his spine; it felt like it was coming from everywhere at once. Cooper tried to move his legs, but couldn't, the sensation managing to freeze them with apprehension for what felt like far too long.

Billy saw Grayson charging to Rikolf's aid, so he rushed to check on Cooper, who was far closer.

"Cooper, what's wrong?"

"Go on Billy!" Cooper urged, "I feel strange, like something's got me locked here."

Billy looked for anything physical – like chains or other bonds. There was nothing.

"Help the others!" Cooper pleaded. "I'll be fine! Go!"

Billy looked at him one more time, then grunted, nodded, and tore away.

Lobjörn was rearing back an arm, ready to strike Rikolf, still writhing on the ground. Grayson leaped, and as Lobjörn's blow descended, Grayson struck him squarely in the gut. It sent him reeling back as Grayson dropped off to the side.

Billy was racing toward them still; they seemed so close yet far away. That's when he saw it happen in slow, tragic motion.

Rikolf shook his head, having mustered enough strength to spring toward the amulet. Grasping its chain in his jaws, he clamped down around it, and there was a sudden shower of sparks.

Billy watched helplessly as a blast of fire cascaded out of the amulet's metallic disc. They writhed like serpents, and Billy skidded to a halt. The heat was intense, and the flames danced in his tear-sparkled eyes.

Rikolf was in such agony as he let go, then fell away like a crumpled piece of burned parchment; the right side of his body was scorched, some of it black, all of it smoking. The horrible flames slithered around for an instant longer, then as quickly as they had appeared, were gone.

It was then that Cooper's legs were suddenly free to move, as if the heat of that unnatural fire had melted those unseen restraints. He rushed toward them all, heart in his chest and head pounding. Taking up a position next to Grayson, the two of them watched Billy hunch over the dreadful sight of Rikolf's smoking body. Tears were falling.

"Pathetic," said Lobjörn, miraculously unburned. "The Vermilion pack relying on whelps to do the work their Alpha can't."

Billy turned, his roared filled with intense anger, rivaling the fires which were no more.

Cooper pointed a long finger toward the Bear King. "Quiet, Yogi! Now hand that amulet over while you still can."

Lobjörn laughed the demand off. "Pathetic little threats now? Please! Just who do you think you are?"

Grayson took a step back as Cooper advanced.

The Alpha's eyes once again flashed with an emerald fervor. "Weren't you listening earlier?" he said. "We're your undoing…"

There came a sound like thunder, Billy storming the Bear King from the side.

Boom!

"Oh, and I forgot to add that things might get a little dire…"

Billy roared again, cutting Lobjörn's stomach deep.

Cooper lunged, his own claws connecting, then swiping along the side of Lobjörn's face.

As Grayson prepared to join the battle, he heard feet approaching. They were running, and as he turned around, he saw that Alyssa rushing at him.

"It was a close call," she told him as she arrived, "but most of the ships made it into the Bay."

"That's good news indeed," he replied, eyes sinking from hers toward his brother-in-law. "This, on the other hand is bad, Alyssa. Really bad."

"Oh my God, what happened?" With a horrified look in her eyes, Alyssa examined the body and saw that the wounds were still smoldering yet, miraculously, Rikolf was still breathing. "We need to get him to a healer, immediately! There's still a chance we can save him."

"But Alyssa, they are now on the ships that have set sail into the Bay, are they not?"

Alyssa nodded, crestfallen by the reality of things.

"Wait. There is still a chance. Do you still have any of the things I gave you earlier?" Grayson asked hopefully.

Alyssa's hand darted to the outside of her front pocket, feeling. "I do, but oh no," she answered, her face scrunched and stomach churning.

"It's either that or we physically drag him all the way across camp, then swim to one of those boats."

Alyssa gazed through the chaos behind her, across the burning camp, and out across the water in an attempt to rationalize that it was somehow doable. It wasn't.

"Okay, okay," she agreed, and huffing, plunged a hand into her pocket.

Alyssa pulled out what looked like another transportation stone, this one smaller than the one that had gotten them all the way from Georgia to Louisiana, but she assumed that it would be no less unpleasant. She took a very deep breath, which did nothing to calm her nerves.

"On the count of three then?" Grayson asked, adding, "It'll be much better for you this time. Just think of the healer's vessel. The stone will do the rest."

Not very assured of that, Alyssa placed a hand on Rikolf's body. It was very hot to the touch.

Grayson did the same thing and Alyssa raised her hand high, ready to cast the stone as Grayson counted up.

"One…"

Alyssa breathed out to get ready for the experience.

"Two…"

She closed her eyes, not really ready for the experience at all.

"Three…"

She threw the stone toward the ground, and the three of them vanished in a rush of cool air.

Chapter 19

THE DEVIL'S IRE

1

Billy and Cooper had no idea that Alyssa and Grayson had taken Rikolf to safety, their full focus and combined might poured into toppling the Bear King, or outright killing him. Cooper did not have to ask Billy which option he'd prefer, the ferocity of the dire wolf's blows and the unwillingness to give Lobjörn the slightest chance to escape, never mind breathe, was apparent.

Yet despite the full brunt of Billy's powerful blows and tremendous bites, Lobjörn would not yield nor fall, Cooper knowing that the infernal thing around the Bear King's neck was what kept him going.

Suddenly the tide shifted, and when Billy went in with hackles raised and claws poised to seize Lobjörn by the scruff of his neck, he was met with a potent blow to both shoulders, the very bones leaving their sockets, buckling, then fracturing along the length to the elbow. Billy screamed, the sound horrid, and he then collapsed.

The Bear King unleashed his fury, and the pummeling reminded Cooper of Derek Wilder beating Billy mercilessly back in 2005, the only thing missing was the alleyway in which it occurred. Regardless, the memory of the first time Billy and he had met burned within him, fueling Cooper's feet, claws, jaws to and then through Lobjörn.

The Bear King let out a cry, grasping his side, and as Cooper looped around for another volley, Lobjörn spun in place. His large fist connected with Cooper's chest, knocking him backwards to tumble head over feet into the mud.

"When are you all going to realize you cannot stop what is coming?" the Bear King said before dropping to his knees. "I am your salvation! I am –"

Lobjörn's voice was suddenly quieted, and Cooper could only hear his own sharp breaths like daggers in his chest, and feel his legs burning with pain. Managing to lift his head, Cooper was surprised to see the man – that demon named Camio from before – standing behind Lobjörn.

There was a nasty, guttural noise like thick water glopping down a drain. It took a moment for Cooper to realize the source, or perhaps he noticed it right away and chose to ignore it. The demon's fist had plowed through the Bear King's throat, clasping the dripping amulet on the other side.

"I agree with that White Wolf," Camio said hatefully. "You really should have read those ancient texts instead of relying on what your prisoner was telling you… under duress."

Lobjörn sputtered something incomprehensible, his eyes wide as the demon pulled the amulet through the hole it had made. The metal disc sparked as if to say goodbye, and Lobjörn was soon engulfed in the same fires that had injured Rikolf so gravely.

There were no screams as Camio withdrew, only sounds of gargling and splashing. Holding the amulet close to his chest, Cooper thought it was strange that the demon didn't just put it on. His red eyes and face almost looked reverent. There was a sound like cracking wood, and before long, the two watched as Lobjörn's body collapsed on itself, tumbling to the floor in a pile of smoldering ash.

"The pathetic Bear King of the Tensas River Basin is no more", said the new threat now looming on the horizon.

Camio turned to depart, dashing with speed toward the land-bridge. Cooper struggled to rise in an attempt to pursue him, yet as he got to his feet and prepared to run, the demon suddenly stopped just shy of the crossing. Camio's body was convulsing – as it had earlier by Lobjörn's torture – but this time there was no inherent fear, nor did his screams incite panic and dread within Cooper. No, it was almost euphoric, a blinding white light engulfing the demon's body, shining brightest from his open eyes and gaping mouth.

Cooper could hear a hum, almost choral, and once the light had faded back to the level of morning, Cooper cautiously stepped closer to the steaming body. It was still glowing ever so slightly, and the demon – or what was left of it – was still breathing. Reaching out, Cooper aimed for the amulet but he hesitated, that feeling of dread returning.

Go on... said a distant and soothing voice. *It will be alright. It is your destiny...*

Trusting a voice he did not know, Cooper reluctantly reached out again, and as his fingers grazed the amulet's cold metal, his mind began to unravel and the world around him faded away…

2

Cooper felt weightless in the nothingness that surrounded him. In the darkness of the void, he didn't yet know that he would see things – the same visions of people and places unknown from his dreams – yet with more clarity, and more pain than he had experienced before. Cooper Bennett didn't know it yet, but even a small-town Georgia boy such as himself could be the smallest stone that caused ripples to spread out to affect the whole world.

***

A foul odor like rotten eggs rushes Cooper as he whooshes through a stinging shower of sparks. They cascade over his body, naked under the full moon as he transforms from a boy… to a man… to a wolf.

***

The amulet is hanging low and heavy on Cooper's neck. He looks to the stars above, taking a step on an invisible set of stairs, climbing ever higher as the chain swelters and the disc burns. There is a man-shaped flash of light ahead, so bright he shields it with an arm as the sting of sparks resume.

***

Cities burn across the horizon while packs of feral beasts hunt openly in the streets. It reminds Cooper of Goodman just before Saint Patrick's Day, especially as he steps on a wolf's skull, which cracks then shatters underfoot.

***

Two rings appear out of thin air, spinning. As Cooper tries to grab them, they float just out of his reach. The one on the right is made of platinum entwined gold while on the left, a thin circle of rust is on the verge of falling apart. Cooper is reminded of his own black ring and of Billy's white one.

Oh, Billy…

Cooper hopes that he is okay.

***

Cooper feels a pinch at the nape of his neck and is cinched backwards through a kaleidoscope of sickening colors. He stops on a small island that is set above a thunderstorm; the roiling clouds stretch out for as far as his eyes can see.

Suddenly, the land heaves to and fro. Cooper starts to feel ill, looking up from the rocking horizon. Far above another blanket of storms trembled, sandwiching Cooper in between.

Lightning flings itself from the topmost clouds all the way to the bottom, building in rage until a massive bolt whips free, straight toward Cooper. He leaps out of the way just in time, though the solid rock falls away into the abyss, taking Cooper with it.

***

As Cooper falls and is struck by shards of sharp rocks, he sees things take shape in the swirling debris.

A golden crown, wreathed in flame, is set upon the silhouette of a man. Cooper is reminded of Camio as he turns and ...

(flash)

An army from the Order, comprised of both supernatural and human beings, are locked in a great battle against a legion of demons and...

(flash)

A man with long, black hair turns away, disheartened...

Billy?

(Joey...)

And the faint sounds of a woman's scream rises in his ears...

Alyssa?

(Adrienne...)

Silence cuts through the scream as Cooper realizes the bottom is approaching fast. There is no indication that he's slowing down, and as the hard ground races toward him, Cooper holds out his arms and tries to transform... but the impact is so great that his entire body breaks in one, short thud.

***

As blood trickles and his last few breaths escape in coughs, Cooper sees a hooded figure approaching, wielding a scythe in its ancient hand.

It stops in front of Cooper and looks down through a pair of empty, sunken sockets. "You are not the one for this," it says, bringing the scythe up above its head then down in one fell swoop.

(flash)

Cooper screamed as he flung his eyes open with a terrified quickness, feeling every square inch of his thin body to make sure everything was there and in its proper place.

Without his thick glasses on, he couldn't see well at all, but the blur around him was familiar enough. Cooper was in his bedroom at his father's house, lying on the floor atop one of the three sheets he had for bedding, just like he did every single night of his poor and miserable life in Goodman.

Speaking of his dad, the abusive jerk was skulking about in the kitchen that was just down the short hall outside both their bedrooms. Cooper had to go to the bathroom, which was also in that hallway, but he'd rather hold it in – like his feelings – than face that wretched man more than once a night.

What a weird dream, Cooper thought about instead. *And who were all those people in it? I know Billy, and Alyssa but she looked so different… and…*

A rumble of thunder that sounded like it was just outside his window drew his attention. Getting up, Cooper approached the narrow panes of glass nervously. There were flashes of lightning shining through the blinds – again it was like they were right on the other side. Few in number at first, there was soon a seizure-inducing torrent of light and sound. Using two fingers to separate the blinds, Cooper peered through and saw blurry storm clouds above and below the house.

"What the heck?" he whispered right as a lightning bolt came crashing into the glass.

It shattered and…

(flash)

A hooded man stands in a dusty marketplace, inspecting what looks like the amulet on its chain...

(flash)

Another man that could easily be the last one's son was in a small cellar, picking up the same amulet. Once he did, a massive beam of red light shot high into the sky like a herald...

(flash)

Somewhere distant and dark, a giant firestorm erupts in the middle of an old warehouse, setting the walls alight and causing many people to run. It takes the shape of a horned skull as a woman screens her face from the searing heat of the flames.

A flash of hot silver flies out of the breach with a rumble, the spinning razor finding its way across many necks, bodies toppling.

"No!" the woman shouts shrilly in the orange light. "You cannot be here!"

"But I am here, my dear Onoskelis," replies a foreboding voice. "Now, get out of my way..."

Smoke pours out from the flaming skull, forcing its way into the woman's body by way of her nose and mouth. She looks as though she is choking, a lighter-colored smoke falling to the floor before wafting away in the hot air. All then fades to darkness, except for two blood-red eyes that cast a dim glow on an evil grin.

(flash)

There is a hooded man meeting with Grayson in what looks like the snowy mountains around Goodman. Cooper tries to listen, only hearing bits of the conversation.

But he gets a name…

Ty… Sheridan…

(flash)

Cooper sees Ty again, this time running the streets of some old world city. The place reminds him of France, and as the scene shifts to a great battle at the Eiffel Tower, it is confirmed…

(flash)

A muscular, tattooed man with those red demon eyes is rampaging through a motorcycle club, bodies exploding in horrific and grotesque sprays of gore.

Cooper catches the name of the place off the back of one of the vests – the Snake Eyes MC – and tries to look away as the demon shoves the man wearing it onto a sofa. He places one of the man's fingers into a cigar cutter before…

(flash)

The same demon-man is cavorting with two witches in a dilapidated cabin. After a round of intense intercourse (that Cooper couldn't stomach to watch) he kills one with a crossbow that had been waiting on the walls but spares the other when the warlock falls to his knees.

"I can help you, Master. There is a book I know of that can serve as a backup plan..."

The demon is very interested and with a malevolent smile says, "Tell me more..."

***

Cooper opened his eyes. He was standing on the edge of a cliff in that same infernal place with storms raging above and below.

"Let me out!" he cried, his voice lost in the distant rumbling and bright horizon. "I want to get out! Now!"

Cooper started to cry as the images he'd seen repeated in his mind. The details were even clearer; the blood more wet, the gore more foul, the smells more vile. Driven to the brink of insanity, Cooper peered over the edge and considered jumping to his end.

"Cooper..." He looked up upon hearing the gentle voice, trails of tears streaming down flushed cheeks from his bloodshot eyes. It was Alyssa's voice. "Cooper, come back to us. Please, Cooper, come back."

As she pleaded with him again, a closing book descended from the clouds overhead and another voice – a new voice – came to him just as the pages ignited.

"It is not yet your time, Mr. Bennett. No, that time is yet to come, but the Watcher must now see what must be done to set things right that are now wrong…"

Then, a face appeared in the burning pages. It was that of the man Camio had possessed! He looked to Cooper with malevolence, though perhaps it was more agony, screaming as Cooper once again descended into darkness and despair shouting, "I just want to go home!"

Chapter 20

AN UNIMAGINABLE MEETING

Wednesday April 17, 2013

1

"I just want to go home!" Cooper shouted loud enough to wake himself with a start.

"He's awake!" a relieved voice said. Grayson then appeared at the side of Cooper's bed as he regained some semblance of his feelings and senses. "Cooper? Welcome back. Take your time, my boy."

Cooper looked around the room, the oversaturated colors from his visions fading to reveal a weird yet comfortable space that was like a hospital had merged right with the forest. There were beds growing out of the ground like great leaves, while modern medical equipment and other more magical contraptions were interwoven with twisting bald cypress branches. Above him, little motes of light floated like fairy dust in the air, providing much of the room's illumination.

"Where am I?" Cooper asked, still dazed. He licked his lips. They were dry. "This place feels like a dream."

"Here, take this," Grayson said as he handed him a glass of water. "You are at Avery Island, one of the Aves' outposts closest to Vermilion Bay – about a dozen miles from the camp, give or take. They arrived soon after the fighting started to help those left on shore with the Bear King's forces."

Cooper coughed at the mention, spitting up some water as he remembered Lobjörn's gruesome demise.

"Shh, shh," Grayson shushed. "You'll be alright. Lobjörn is indeed dead, though from what we found I'm not quite sure what lead to his demise."

"It was the amulet," Cooper said, "the same fiery fate that nearly took Rikolf."

It was Grayson's turn to react at the mention of a name. His eyes fell.

"He, he hasn't died too, has he?" Cooper asked with worry.

"No," Grayson said with a sniff, and both men sighed with relief. "Alyssa and Billy are with him."

Cooper tensed and shifted in his bed.

"Not here at Avery Island," Grayson revealed, his hands performing a calming gesture. "They are up at Grand Lake where the healers have access to more advanced supplies and techniques."

Cooper relaxed, sinking into the soft mattress – or whatever it was he was laying on. "How long has it been since the battle?"

Grayson did a quick mental calculation; it made Cooper nervous. "It's been three days."

"What?" Cooper exclaimed, then tensed up even more. "Three days!"

Grayson nodded.

"I can't believe it," Cooper replied. "No wonder I thought I was going insane, though I am glad 'only' three days passed out here. It felt like much, much longer in there."

"What do you mean 'in there'?" Grayson asked. "Your dreams?"

Cooper nodded, telling Grayson everything that he saw. Most of it was unknown to him, Cooper could tell by his expressions, but once Cooper made mention of his meeting with Ty Sheridan, Grayson's face changed. He looked worried, and amazed.

"So you saw this man, Ty Sheridan in your visions?" Grayson asked.

"Yes, you were both up in the mountains. Looked like Goodman or thereabouts. It was snowing…"

"… in January 2012," Grayson added. "That was before you were involved with anything wolf-related, beyond Liam of course. How is this possible, Cooper?"

He shrugged then flopped his hands down to his sides. "Your guess is as good as mine Grayson."

"Well, I think you and I would agree, Cooper, that if what you saw happening with me is true, then the rest of it should very well be considered reality, a very frightening reality."

Cooper heard substantial footsteps approaching. Glancing over, he saw a huge, beastly man standing there with arms like tree trunks and a chest and back that seemed as broad as he was tall. For a split second his heart seized up, thinking that Lobjörn had been reincarnated, but upon further inspection, once he realized it was someone else, he settled down.

"Cooper, let me introduce you to Svarbjörn, the Bear King of the Atchafalaya River Basin. A true king and friend if this region ever had one."

"My pleasure," Cooper said, extending a hand.

"The same," Svarbjörn replied, taking it to shake. His hand was massive, enveloping Cooper's with ease. "How are you holding up?"

"Good, I think," Cooper replied. "All things considered."

"Great to hear," Svarbjörn said. "I wish we all had the luxury of time to recover one-hundred percent, but there are reports coming in from the east that demons are on the move, fast, and that they are coming here. I suppose the couple of times their trinket was used made them worry and pick up the pace, especially now that they know we have it, or rather that you have it, Cooper Bennett."

Cooper didn't even realize that he was wearing the amulet, but sure enough there it was around his neck when he checked.

"Speaking of demons, is that man, Camio, still alive?" Cooper asked, a sudden flash of the screaming face from his dreams invading his mind.

"The foul thing is gone," answered Svarbjörn, much to Cooper's disappointment. However, Svarbjörn continued. "But something else has replaced it within that man's body."

Unsure what that meant, Cooper asked, "Has he, um, *it* told you anything?"

"No," Svarbjörn replied bearishly, and Grayson shook his head too.

"The only thing it has said is that it will speak to the 'Watcher,'" Grayson added, "but we have no idea who or what that is."

Cooper gasped, dropping the glass of water as he remembered the last of his dream.

The Watcher must now see what must be done to set things right that are now wrong...

"I think... I think that Watcher could be me..."

2

While the lands surrounding Avery Island were covered by bayous, swampland, and marshes, beneath it was a large dome of rock salt. Used primarily for mining and manufacture, deep in the mines the Aves had also fashioned a storage facility due to the natural environment, which provided a consistent year-round temperature and humidity level – ideal for the preservation of paper, film, art, and artifacts. Over the years, some of those areas were also converted into chambers to house criminals and other supernatural beings, the natural properties of salt once again being used for its mystical containment and repelling powers.

Later that Wednesday, once Cooper had the chance to get bathed and something to eat, Grayson and Svarbjörn accompanied him under Avery Island to one of its deepest holding cells, simply known as the Salt Box.

The descent into the mines seemed to take forever, Cooper trying to see beyond the narrow slits and holes of the grates around him. Pressed up against the cold metal – since there wasn't much space in the elevator to begin with and Svarbjörn's bulk took up way more than his fair share – the view wasn't much more than dull gray walls lit by passing orange lamps mounted to the elevator shaft. Although the scenery was quite boring, the feeling Cooper couldn't shed was ominous – like he was in a coffin and that was being lowered into a grave; the deepest grave ever.

After endless minutes, the elevator slowed, creaked and groaned, then finally stopped. Once its doors opened, Cooper felt as if a giant weight had been lifted off him (quite literally) and he staggered out of the lift into a massive chamber. The sheer scale of the mines became evident as Cooper looked around to gain his bearings, the tall walls rising high and forming tunnels that extended in three directions – left, right, and straight ahead – all well past the light of more lamps as they plunged into darkness.

"This way," Grayson said, walking down the centermost path toward the last set of lights.

There was a door made out of a solid block of salt, mounted to the walls by means of huge iron fixtures. Cooper imagined something easily punching its way through the door – thinking it was just like the salt shakers at Castillo's – but when he knocked on it, he found it to be as hard as granite.

"Even a bear shifter would have trouble cracking these doors," Svarbjörn noted, "and since most other supernatural beings have an aversion to salt, they pretty much stay where placed in the room."

"I couldn't imagine not having salt as part of my diet, never mind being scared of it, though I'm sure my friend Dr. Ross would disagree," Cooper said with a laugh, and as Grayson swung the heavy door inward, Svarbjörn chuckled too.

"Come, gentlemen, it is time," Grayson said, entering the room after surveying the entryway with a few quick glances.

As Cooper walked inside, the air felt warmer – even though he knew the temperature down there should be the same no matter where they were. The room was empty except for more dim lights in the corners, catching the odd cascade of loose salt tumbling like delicate wisps of cloud. Then he saw Camio standing to face them, or his body at least, anchored to the salt floor with iron restraints. Etched in the salt was a large circle with a star inside, and a few words of Latin rimmed the edges of the symbol.

"Hello?" Cooper said with caution. He stepped closer but decided to not get *too* close. Once he could make out the details on the man's face (no easy task considering how subdued the lights were), he stopped.

"Ah, the Watcher is awake at last," the man said.

Cooper thought the voice was far less menacing than Camio's but, in some strange way, more powerful. He wasn't sure how that was possible.

"Camio?" Cooper asked.

"No," the man replied.

"Then, what is your name?"

He smiled loosely, wrinkling his brow with a single eyebrow raise as if trying to remember. "I think my name was Chance…"

"Chance?"

"Yes, Chance… Wilcox…" The man's voice was bewildered. "At least I think that is what this vessel was called in a former life, but in this one you may address me as… Seraphiel."

I can see what Billy meant by all these weird names, Cooper thought to himself. "Vessel?" he asked. "What exactly are you?"

"A Watcher such as yourself, but, to put this in terms you are more inclined to understand, you might know my kind as angels."

"Of course," Svarbjörn said sarcastically. Then he grumbled, moving to rest his back against the end of the open door. He crossed his arms. "We've got the demons already, so we might as well get the matching set."

"My role is to ensure things are as they should be," Seraphiel continued, "as recorded by Metatron, the highest of my order, the Celestial Scribe. It would seem that things here on Earth are *not* as they should be. Your visions for example, Cooper Bennett, are of things that have happened before, yet will never come to pass."

Cooper's expression betrayed any understanding that he might have had about what Seraphiel was talking about.

"So, are you saying that something has changed from the things this Metatron had recorded as history?" asked Grayson, apparently having more of an understanding of the situation than Cooper.

I hereby nominate you as the Watcher, Cooper thought flippantly.

"Yes," Seraphiel replied to Grayson. "In short, the Grand Demon Dajjal, who was once a servant of Lucifer before he betrayed him, has found a way to escape his ultimate defeat at the hands of the Order of Journeymen. It is a perversion that must be rectified."

"But… how?" Cooper thought, clueless. "I mean, I only found out about shifters less than a year ago, so I'm no expert on all this paranormal stuff."

"None of us are," Svarbjörn replied inconsolably, "yet here we are nonetheless."

"So how do you, I mean Chance, play into all of this?" Grayson asked.

Seraphiel sat down on the floor.

"Dajjal was able to return here using a book that this body – Chance's body – was trapped inside. Those witches that you saw briefly in your visions, Cooper, they had access to it and its dark magic. When Chance was imprisoned on October 19, 2012, fragments of his memories were scattered through its pages, which I assumed he was using in some way to help himself manifest again. Since Chance's personality had remained intact and those memories were from a specific, and early enough time, it was a perfect route for Dajjal to take back here when things did not go well for him during his final assault. "

"This is a lot to process," Cooper said, also sitting down. He licked a finger, swiped the floor, and popped it in his mouth. Grayson stuck his tongue out in disgust.

"When one meddles with things at this level, a clear understanding is often the last thing to arrive," Seraphiel said. "All I know is that destiny has placed the amulet and chain in your possession, Cooper. I believe it should have come back with Dajjal as part of his plan, but instead it ended up here at a later time by some cosmic fortune."

"Which explains the sudden changes in Lobjörn's actions around February," said Svarbjörn.

"Precisely," Seraphiel agreed, "and Dajjal must not get the amulet before a man named Gage Crosse. If he does, then all will indeed be lost."

Cooper jumped to his feet. "Then let's find this Gage guy and give it to him."

"No," Seraphiel said. "It is too early for that to happen. You must hide the amulet until the time is right, even though that will be risky and demons will be on your trail. But yet, I fear that even if he were to get it *when* he should, the circumstances leading to its discovery would have changed *why* he should. That could also be catastrophic."

"I saw a man that looked like his father, how about him?"

Seraphiel shook his head again. "We cannot give it to Charles now."

"So, what you are saying is we are all fucked," Svarbjörn grunted curtly. "As much as I like a good romp, that is not something I wanted to hear."

Seraphiel closed his eyes and shook his head. "We must tread very, very carefully. Everything is already out of balance and should the scales tip any more, I fear we may awaken the First."

Svarbjörn shifted his position at the door. "I don't suppose that would be a good thing."

Seraphiel looked grave, replying, "That would be the *worst* thing."

Seraphiel then looked toward Cooper and spoke to him without moving his lips; his voice was between their minds only.

"The others cannot hear this. Whatever happens with the coming Night, I need you to promise, as Watcher, that you stay the course until the time is right. Do you understand?"

Cooper didn't fully comprehend, but nodded anyway. He suspected Seraphiel had something planned, though he didn't know what it was.

"Yet you will know, Cooper, when the time is right. Until then, remember: Stay. The. Course…"

"This is all so confusing," Cooper sighed, looking to Grayson as he walked up to him. Leaning in, he whispered, "I feel like I should check in to the loony bin."

"You and me both," Grayson replied with the smallest smile. "So, do you actually believe all this?"

"I'm not sure, but those visions were pretty clear. Besides, I like the idea of these demons losing versus Hell being on Earth."

Seraphiel remained silent as Grayson agreed. "I liked it better when all I had to worry about is what Liam was going to have me spend money fixing next."

"I'm with you. I miss those days. So, I guess it's up to us to watch over this amulet now," Cooper said hesitantly, looking down at the plain-looking thing.

"Indeed," Seraphiel said. "It is up to you. Remember to watch over it with your life, as fate rests on your shoulders young man, and the Great Demon will do his best knock you, and all else, down to ruin."

"Great," Cooper replied. "Absolutely no pressure at all."

Chapter 21

MOMENTS OF TRANSITION

Wednesday April 24, 2013

1

Over the next week, Svarbjörn led the preparations for the imminent demon attack against Louisiana. The past days had been relatively calm, but with so much to worry about and do, the Bear King knew that the quiet was a sign that things were on the verge of getting really nasty. It was the calm before the proverbial – made physical – storm.

A startling amount of demon signs had been seen on the far fringes of the state, mainly in the east as lightning storms during perfectly clear days. Calling on the other clans to help, and in order to minimize collateral damage to their respective territories (both material and loss of life), Svarbjörn declared The Gathering draw the line at Honey Island and the Pearl River on the border with Mississippi. That would place them ahead of the most active demon front, where they would hopefully be able to stop the infernal tide and save themselves from destruction.

2

Cooper sat on a grassy hilltop in his wolf form, Alyssa tucked into the comfortable space between his elbow and chest, rubbing his hair gently while his body rose and fell with each breath. Billy was with them, though situated near Cooper's tail eating a bag of gummy bears. The three of them were watching the sun sink toward the horizon beyond Slidell, the city of New Orleans glittering a little further to the south. They weren't there for any grand purpose or to devise battle strategies. They were just there to be around each other and talk.

"How can you still eat those things?" Cooper asked Billy, watching him shove another handful of sweets into his mouth.

"I don't know, I just can," Billy replied, mouth almost bursting as he struggled to chew.

"But you know people that look like that," Cooper retorted. "I can't look at them and not think of Svarbjörn."

Alyssa snickered at the notion of Cooper associating a tiny gummy bear with a massively muscled, hairy man. She could barely get her next words out for her giggles. "Is that why you can't eat bacon and eggs anymore too?"

Billy joined in with her laughter. "No way," he said. "Coop, they still taste the same."

"Whatever guys… not to me."

"I will say," Alyssa started, "that being a shifter isn't anything like I thought it would be. It's far less romantic and far more tragic."

Billy sighed and Cooper looked over, spotting him looking at his tail. He wondered if Billy was thinking about Rikolf.

"Real life often isn't as cut and dry, or nice and pretty as everyone would have you believe," Cooper said, "and often the ones saying that it is are doing something shady to make their lives easier. At least it feels that way. I sometimes wonder if there is anything good left in this world."

Alyssa rubbed his chest with her nails. "I would argue there is," she said, "and that I'm looking at one of them right now."

Cooper smiled, filled with the feeling that she was right. To him, she was one of the most precious things out there.

Billy coughed, then sniffled.

"You holding up okay, buddy?" Cooper asked.

"Yeah," Billy said, then immediately shook his head. "Just thinking about Rikolf's injuries… and our luck. Here it is we both finally find something that makes us happy and the universe decides to take a great big dump on it."

Alyssa sat up and cast him a reassuring glance. "Oh, Billy… Rikolf's injuries were pretty severe, but it looks promising that he's going to recover over time. I mean, it's been ten days or so since Lobjörn's attack but Rikolf's healing more each day. You've got a fighter of a man, Billy, just like you are."

Billy smiled back at Alyssa. "Thank you."

"Always, William."

"Looking at the positive, he's also been too weak to shift multiple times, which might speed up the process when he can," Cooper added. "And the fact his wounds stopped burning after that first shift back to human form was a good thing."

"A *great* thing," Alyssa underscored.

"Yeah, you're right. Especially since I don't think that was ordinary fire," Billy said as he stuffed his mouth full of more gummies.

Alyssa laughed, more at the sight of him with those ballooned cheeks rather than the obvious statement.

"Nope," Cooper agreed. "Last time I checked grandma's necklaces didn't spew tendrils of living fire. Your butt after Mexican food though comes pretty close."

Billy threw a gummy bear his way; Cooper caught it midair and ate it.

"You think that Dr. Ross might be able to help him? Like he did you?"

Cooper sighed. "I… I'm not sure. Maybe you can ask him when we get back to Goodman."

There was a long pause. Even the birds and beasts had stopped their nightly symphony.

"I was hoping that you could ask him for me." Billy's words crept out of his mouth so slowly Cooper thought he had misheard.

"Why would I ask him?" Cooper questioned. "You're going to be there with us, right?"

"I think… I'm going… to stay."

Cooper's face became full of emotion, even showing through his wolf muzzle. "You can't be serious?"

"I most definitely am," Billy replied confidently.

"You can't…"

"You've seen the other wolves back home, Coop. Me being there is a problem. A big one, especially for you."

Sniffling, Cooper looked his way with glistening green eyes. "Billy, you can't stay here."

"Why? Because you say I can't?"

"What? No," Cooper replied defensively. "It's because I'll…"

"Cooper…" Alyssa said softly.

Dammit, her words are always so calming.

"Stop. Billy, is this what you really want?" she asked.

Billy hesitated, his eyes struggling to find a resting spot. He chose a pebble on the ground nearby and took a deep breath. "Yes."

"Then there's nothing more to discuss."

"I…" Cooper began, but Alyssa's eyes looked up to him and sparked with the same emerald fire in his own.

"We'll support you Billy," Alyssa reassured. "Right, Coop?

Cooper began to stand, repositioning himself to sit next to Billy. Alyssa stood back with her arms crossed, watching and waiting for him to lash out. But Cooper didn't do anything of the sort that night. Instead, he simply sat there next to Billy, saying, "Family always supports each other."

Alyssa smiled, and sitting beside Cooper she grabbed his arm tightly. Her head found a soft spot on his side. Billy also leaned into Cooper, and the trio looked out across Louisiana with heavy hearts held by uplifted souls.

"I love you guys," Billy said.

Then, as if called to action to test that love, the distant east sky came alive with lightning, and the smell of sulfur was faint on the wind.

"Demons?" Billy asked, as they all stood and turned.

"No doubt," Cooper replied, and the three friends ran toward trouble, as they always did, with each other.

Chapter 22

NIGHT FALLS ON THE BAYOU

1

The time The Gathering prepared for and feared had arrived, the demonic forces of the Noctis pouring into the dark lands of Louisiana just after sunset on April 24, 2013. The eastern sky was ablaze with lightning and fire, the ground trembling for miles under the assault of countless sprinting feet.

Clad in a ceremonial corslet of intersecting golden plates, Svarbjörn stood ahead of a great host of animals comprised of shifters from across the state and beyond. Bears were there, from both the Atchafalaya and Tensas River basins, boars from ten Soundries across Louisiana and Texas, and mighty eagles from across the southern skies. Also present were what few wolves remained from Vermilion Bay, supported by their brothers in the White and Shadow Wolf packs all the way from the Blue Ridge Mountains.

It was a grand sight, and all eyes on the ground and above were on the Bear King as he spoke.

"Thank you, all my friends, for coming together at this desperate hour. As you can feel through the shuddering ground beneath us, see in the shattered skies above us, and smell across the air between, danger is upon us and it does not care if we have feathers or fur, muzzles or snouts, nor what lineage we descend from or claim as right. They only care that we are alive and they want us dead. It gives me hope for this battle, and for our futures, that we have been able to put aside our differences to face this threat that stares us down. None of the old clans - be they aves, boar, bear, or wolf - is out of their reach. The Demons of the Night have come for blood – all our blood – and we have no choice but to make a stand!"

Those gathered began to roar, a few distinct sounds coming from around the group.

"We will not back down…"

The sound rose as more joined in.

"We will not surrender…"

The roars were now loud, feeding off each other and growing like a boulder tumbling in an avalanche.

"And as my dear friend Rikolf, Alpha of Vermilion Bay once said, and does today in spirit: WE… WILL… SAY… NO…!"

The roars were mighty, coalescing into a unified sound that managed to overcome the demonic thunder that boomed in the distance.

"Now is our time to shine!" Svarbjörn called. "Charge!"

***

The Noctis, ravenous for death, appeared out of a shower of lightning and fire, rushing westward across the marshes toward the allied shifters. The line of possessed humans and rougarou charged like a thunderous tidal wave, rolling over everything ahead while leaving destruction in its wake. Meanwhile, Svarbjörn, focused, led the bear assault eastward to meet them, his contingent of Defenders the first to clash against the demons in a discordant symphony of guttural roars and demonic screams that filled the air with both triumph and loss.

The hellish creatures were much stronger than their human appearance suggested. Some were able to land punches that could maim or break bones in a single strike – even through armor – while others teamed up to force bears on their backs before crushing them with rocks, their fists, or impaling them on broken trees.

The bears were no pushovers either, their sizable bulk and equal resolve sending rows upon rows of demons tumbling through the air in a single, sprinting charge. As demonic bodies came to rest,

Svarbjörn and others would finish them off, his progress stopped when an immense fist struck him across the back. Knocked to the ground, he twisted, spying a gigantic foot plunging toward his head. Svarbjörn rolled, evading death in the nick of time, the foot splashing into the dirt behind him. With the ground quaking, the Bear King looked up and saw that it was a Sasquatch. Driven by fury, and with a single, ruthless move, the bear rolled again and smashed his reinforced fist through the beast's shins. It toppled as he rose, placing the Sasquatch's neck firmly between his jaws. Then, Svarbjörn bit down, and after seconds of squirming and a repulsive *crunch*, the entire body went limp, and was dropped with a *thud*.

Further north along the battlefield, surrounded by awful screams, clamorous noises, and squelching sensations underfoot, Billy and Alyssa were engaged with a pack of ruthless, werewolf-like rougarou.

"Billy, to your right!" Alyssa shouted across her shoulder while she sidestepped a lunging bite, her hindquarters twirling and kicking the feral beast away.

"Thanks!" he growled. Turning and swatting, he landed a blow right between the attacking beast's eyes, getting a full blast of its stench. "Jesus these things stink to high Heaven!"

"Grayson says that they're a lot like wolf shifters," Alyssa hollered, snatching a charging one by the arm and pitching it to the side, "but that each shift degrades their minds until the beast fully takes control."

"Ah, makes sense!" Billy said as he darted between attacking claws, snatching a rougarou by the ankle and dragging it along the marshland. "Now I know why wolf shifters are insulted if you call them one! I'll have to remember that!" Lifting the squirming creature with both arms, he threw it at three more that were dashing toward him.

Billy looked for Alyssa in the turmoil, seeing her handle herself quite well with a series of acrobatic flips and kicks.

"You're getting pretty good with those!" he called.

"Practice makes perfect," she said while making a landing.

Suddenly, several rougarou leapt onto Billy from behind, Alyssa hurrying to his aid. When she got there, scraping the beasts off him like engorged ticks off their prey's skin, they became surrounded.

"Well, this looks like fun," Billy observed as he and Alyssa stood side by side, the rougarou horde encircling, threatening, hungry.

That's when two rougarou bodies suddenly fell from the sky, smashing into the ground between the two groups.

Alyssa and Billy looked upward, and their spirits were lifted when they both saw Warryn and Theryn above, diving down with their talons outstretched, and a flock of other eagles and falcons at their wingtips.

Billy regarded the rougarou horde again, noticing they were no longer threatening but panicked. "Really sucks to be you today!"

Grayson and Cooper lead their respective wolf packs across the swamp, a vastly different sight than what occurred beneath the trees in the Blue Ridge Mountains of 1994. Instead of attacking each other due to their differences or hate, the sea of black and white wolves stormed their dark-hearted enemies with one bright, unified wolf heart.

"Cooper!" Grayson shouted above thundering paws, "this is what family is all about!"

Cooper smiled back across the packs, and nodded.

The shimmering arrow of black and white fur soared across the marshlands, plunging into the incoming line of darkness with one formidable blast. Bones shattered to the left, skin ripped to the right, and demons and rougarou fell beneath the combined will of the White Wolf and Shadow Wolf packs.

As Cooper fought beside his own, he observed demons and shifters alike running in all directions, most with targets in sight, but others were tending to the wounded, to friends, or family; trying to drag bodies that were too heavy away, or getting felled themselves in the process. He felt yanked in ten-thousand different directions without focus, wanting to help them all, and kill them all, yet knowing he could not do it all.

Then, like most things, as soon as it all seemed to begin, there came a silence, aside from heavy breathing, wheezing, and fits of coughing. The conflict appeared to be over, and the group collected themselves in the passing quiet, at least until…

2

A second wave of shapes rushed out of the darkness in fire and lightning, stepping over and onto the casualties from the first wave that were already scattered around the marshes.

Across the whole field of battle, things took an immediate turn for the worse.

Several sizable demons came at Grayson, knocking him to the ground as one that wielded an immense silver axe loomed overhead.

Alyssa tried to evade an incoming dagger. As the silver blade entered her side (she just wasn't fast enough to avoid it), she collapsed to the ground, and Cooper rushed in, forlorn, to her aid. In his state of distraction, three possessed werewolves managed to overwhelm him, all trying to end the Alpha's life by inflicting terrible gashes wherever they would go, and there was a lot of space where they could.

Billy hastened toward his wounded friends, kicking, striking, smashing, and pushing anything and anyone that dared to get in his way.

Grayson watched helplessly as his attacker lifted that large axe up and over his head, preparing to strike. He tried to move away, but the mud was deep, keeping his movements too slow.

Beneath the trio of possessed werewolves and their insatiable claws, Cooper struggled to stay conscious. Hot and sticky blood rushed into his eyes, nose, and mouth, and as he tasted that (*delicious*) bitter metal, the amulet chittered, so softly at first it was no more than a whisper, but soon with such voracity that Cooper had no choice but to reach for it, grab it, yank it from his neck, and hold it aloft. He gained new strength as the amulet began to glow, the werewolves on him fleeing in terror as a powerful jet of red light shot into the sky. Yet it did not stay red, changing quickly to white, then to green. Cooper's eyes glowed brighter than the sun, and his body – changing back into human form – trembled under the weight of the power clenched in his fist.

Grayson was in awe at the sight, yet his demonic attacker did not sway. As the axe fell, he could see the death stroke coming for him with the speed of a bullet, and suddenly Grayson's vision became a gruesome maroon splash while horrific screams filled his ears.

But it was not his blood, nor his screams. The attackers had been stopped by something that can only be described as… magical.

In a swell of mud and water, alligators surged from the marshlands, splashing and roaring around Cooper. They took on the shapes of tall, twisted men with glowing yellow eyes, and as if commanded by the will of The Gathering, the reptilian men attacked the foul creatures with such power they had no defense against it.

"My God," Grayson said in sheer awe, his jaw unable to stay closed. "They're shifters!"

Then, behind the reptilian advance, a mighty stag appeared from the darkness. It stood tall, and its entwined antlers looked like the branches of a tremendous cypress tree. Within those woody folds, flowers bloomed and birds nested, and as the dim petals fell to the ground, thorny vines sprung from their rippling wake and Will-o'-the-wisps came dancing across the bayou. All tore into the heart of the oncoming darkness as if it were nothing more than paper, sending it back to the abyss from where it came.

Cooper, nearly healed from the amulet's strange green herald, staggered over to Alyssa, helping her to her feet. She had shifted back into human form as well, the dagger that had injured her stuck upright in the mud beside them.

"We should keep that as a souvenir," she told him.

"You want to remember getting stabbed tonight?" Cooper asked facetiously.

Alyssa looked back to the dagger and shook her head, instead taking the amulet out of Cooper's hand to put back on his neck. "This is enough of a reminder for us all."

Cooper looked around, and he drew Alyssa to him in an embrace. Svarbjörn's and the shifter army, rallied by the sight of whatever legend had come to their rescue that night, surged forward, routing the lingering darkness to the brink of the marshes.

Yet that fleeting splinter of time, when the threat seemed vanquished and good had truly triumphed over evil, is precisely when the world that they knew was torn apart…

Chapter 23

THE GRAND DEMON

1

As Cooper held Alyssa in his arms, and everything seemed at the point he could finally lower his defenses, the very air itself was rent in a mighty explosion. Knocking Cooper and Alyssa back, the massive wall of fire tore through the retreating demon army and those pursuing them, friend and foe alike collapsing in singed heaps.

As Cooper gazed in horror at the sight, not knowing if Svarbjörn or any of the others were still alive, he saw the dark figure of a man through the flames surging in front of him. Overcome with a tremendous sense of disgust at the realization of who was approaching, Cooper tried to move but found himself frozen again.

"No… not again!" he cried.

Dajjal stepped out of the shadows, wielding a flaming sword and whip. The light illuminated the shape of a bearded, athletic man wearing part of a high-dollar suit that could have been purchased at any of the stores Grayson would frequent.

Grayson! Where are you? Oh my God... Cooper thought frantically, unable to see him. Only Alyssa and Billy were nearby; both unconscious.

With no tie or jacket, and his shirt sleeves rolled up, Cooper could tell Dajjal's vessel was covered in tattoos not unlike Lance's, but instead of black and white, his were full color.

Without a word, Dajjal suddenly advanced, the speed at which he was covering ground petrifying. The alligator men attacked him, but Dajjal was able to keep them back, his weapons cutting through their flesh with the same ease the alligator men had cut though his own army. Cooper noticed that during his attacks and defenses, Dajjal's eyes never once left the amulet around his neck.

Cooper struggled to move but was still firmly locked in place. "Dammit!" he screamed as Dajjal was now mere feet away from him.

Suddenly, the stag sprinted in between them, blocking the demon's advance. Rearing up, the majestic creature struck Dajjal in the chest with one of its hooves, the great demon falling flat on his back.

Angered, Dajjal lashed the creature with his whip, its thong wrapping around the spirit's neck.

"Nooooo!" Cooper cried as Dajjal flicked his wrist, causing the whip to surge with fire, cleaving the beautiful creature's head clean off.

It spun through the air and splashed into the nearby water, crumbling most of the magical defenses that had appeared with its arrival. The area around the head and body became rank with an oily sheen, and the air grew cold despite the fires.

"You pathetic fool," Dajjal said. "Did you really think you could stop my symphony from playing across the world? If the Journeymen and all their resources could not defeat me, how well did you expect one lonely, loser of a boy from a backwoods town to do against a Lord, no, a GOD?"

"Pretty good," Cooper said. "I mean, you are here now, because of me."

Dajjal came closer, stepping over the stag's already decaying corpse.

"I think that we all need challenges in life, don't you?" Cooper continued. "Otherwise how do we ever grow?"

"Only those who rule need do that," Dajjal said, slithering up to Cooper. He was now directly over him, flaming sword at the ready.

"*True* leaders can see that potential in *everyone*," Cooper replied.

Dajjal looked down at Cooper without pity or mercy, yet Cooper did not look away. Dajjal raised the sword above his head. "As I once told some other pathetic thing, there are those who are meant to rule and others who, like you and the rest of this little band of animals, are made to suffer!"

But before Dajjal could deliver the blow, the sword grew brighter (only then did Cooper turn away) and it shattered.

"You always have been so full of yourself," said Seraphiel, who had appeared nearby – close, yet not too close to either of them.

"What are you doing here, angel?"

"Trying to clean up this little… or rather large mess you have made."

Dajjal laughed. "Please, when will you learn I am destined to do this?"

"Well, Dajjal, an important lesson in life is that we all must learn when to give up, and when to *stay your course*." Seraphiel cast an astute look in Cooper's direction.

"Now come," Seraphiel said as he strode up to Dajjal. "Put down your remaining weapon and stop this foolishness."

You're too close! Cooper thought frantically, wishing he could move. *Stay the course? What bullshit!*

As Seraphiel reached out a hand, the demon cracked his whip at the angel, who promptly extinguished it before it transformed into a snake that slithered off into the night.

"Even your weapons are leaving you. Perhaps now we can discuss things more civilly," Seraphiel said to Dajjal, but as he turned to nod at Cooper, the treacherous demon stabbed him in the back with an enchanted blade he took out of his pocket. He broke the end inside Seraphiel's body.

"If you recall," Dajjal said bitterly, "for I know it was recorded, there were angels at my last party, so I certainly came prepared to discuss things 'more civilly' this time."

Seraphiel struggled to stand, falling into the muck. Yet instead of screaming, or begging for his life, the angel smiled as he said, "Just like I came ready to talk to one of the most treacherous demons of all time. Mr. Bennett, NOW!"

Cooper discovered that he could move again, and instinctively jumped to his feet and grabbed hold of the amulet like he had during the attack. Suddenly, his eyes began to glow bright red, the air surging with building energy.

"Give that to me boy!" Dajjal demanded. "I will not let it stay in the hands of an insufferable human any longer!"

"But you know I'm not a human," Cooper countered, his red eyes becoming green as he shifted into his beast form. "I'm an Alpha!"

Dajjal scoffed. "You're an *animal*!"

The two charged, hitting, punching, and cutting each other under the night sky as fires burned the marshlands beyond. Cooper clawed at Dajjal's chest, receiving an equal level of punishment to the side of his own face. Then, with one powerful strike to the gut, Dajjal sent Cooper crashing into the ground, and weakened, he transformed back to a human. The demon wasted no more time and was on the boy quickly, one hand firmly around Cooper's neck while the other was just about to take hold of the amulet.

All seemed on the brink of loss, until one sound changed everything: "Ahem."

"Dajjal," Seraphiel muttered, standing as blood sigils covered his arms and chest. "It was a good try."

Dropping Cooper and the amulet at once, Dajjal charged the angel. The look on his face was pure fear, the fear of failure for the second time.

Seraphiel then touched his hands to his chest, unfurled his wings (now visible and pure), then winked at Cooper while he said the phrase, "*Ab aeterno…*"

Cooper watched as Dajjal crashed into Seraphiel, a white light spilling out from them to cover all the surrounding lands.

Chapter 24

FULL CIRCLE

1

The bright lights and noise of battle faded away to reveal the sights and sounds of a dusty bazaar. Cooper rubbed his eyes and looked around, finding himself in a narrow alleyway, just off a set of streets jam-packed with wares, crates, barrels, and people. There were men of all shapes, sizes, and attire crossing the mouth of the alley, alongside women who were veiled in black. In the distance were soaring minarets along the jagged outline of an olden skyline, while the air was filled with warmth and the smell of exotic spices.

Psst, came a sound to Cooper's left.

He spun his head around and saw that Alyssa and Billy were huddled behind a stack of trunks and clothing racks.

"Cooper!" Billy shout-whispered. "Get over here!"

Looking down, Cooper remembered that he was naked except for the amulet around his neck, and promptly scurried over to his two friends.

"Do you have any idea where we are?" Cooper asked.

Billy shook his head, saying, "No, but I'd guess quite a long way from home."

"I have an idea," Alyssa said, her expression suggesting she was close to figuring out exactly where.

"Good, because I'm not recognizing anything right off," Cooper said, "and I haven't seen Grayson, or anyone else we know for that matter."

"Cooper, is this similar to any of the visions you've had?" Alyssa asked.

"Visions?" Billy repeated, unaware Cooper had had any at all.

"It feels familiar," Cooper replied, turning to Billy. "With all the stress of things recently, I didn't want to pile the fact I was heading toward a mental institution on top of your list of things."

Billy shrugged it off. "Are we looking for anything special?"

"Not sure yet," Cooper said, still searching.

"It seems to be the next morning," Billy noted, pointing up. "I wonder if our friends… and Rikolf are okay? Considering how the battle was going…"

"I'm sure they all are," Alyssa comforted. "After all, Rikolf was well protected."

Suddenly, Cooper was grabbing some clothes out of one of the open trunks, tossing them to the others.

"Well, well, we're getting quite used to taking clothes from stores aren't we?" Billy observed.

"Hush! Just put these on and fast!

The look on Cooper's face said not to argue, and everyone dressed quickly with the clothes that fit best. Cooper managed to get on some jeans and a plain grey shirt, Billy a soccer tee, while Alyssa was able to find a pair of long pants, long sleeved shirt, and a scarf for her head. None of them had socks or shoes on.

"You look fetching my dear" Billy told Alyssa, and she bowed.

"Shh!" Cooper urged with purpose. "Come on, now that we look… passable… I think I saw the reason we are here. Follow me, we need to catch up."

The ABCs left the isolation of the alley and headed into a sprawling market, falling in behind a confident man in a suit making his way through the bustling area. They passed by colorful vendors that lined the streets selling fine cloth, baskets, jewelry, and pottery. Alyssa was enamored by one particular lantern shop, the colors and designs like artful stained glass. There were street food vendors too, capturing Billy's attention. He could smell things like kebabs and shawarma, along with more traditional dishes like fuul and kushari (though he didn't know their names nor could he read the signs). Baskets overflowed with regional fruits – melons, figs, prickly pears, and dates. It was all such a far cry from Goodman, Georgia, and though they could have stopped to enjoy the rich culture, history, craftsmanship, and tastes, the trio had to press on.

"Who is that?" Alyssa nudged Cooper as they entered a narrow passageway, his feet still leading them along quickly.

"Charles Crosse," Cooper said as if the man were an old friend and Alyssa should have known.

"Who?" Billy asked when they emerged into another bustling area filled with wares. He was struggling to keep his feet from tripping at that pace without shoes.

"He's someone who needs to get this as soon as possible," Cooper revealed, patting the amulet beneath his shirt. "At least, I hope I'm right about that."

As the trio kept up with Charles and his purposeful pace, they tried their best to not look like they were following him. This particular section of the market was less inviting than the last, the men there angrier and leery. There were catcalls to Alyssa which she ignored, and awful stares toward the other two as if they didn't belong.

Billy struggled to not let it bother him, though Cooper was focused, watching Charles as he approached the very market stall from his visions. As he saw Charles looking over the glimmering collection of fine jewelry and other artifacts on display, something dawned on him.

"Shit," Cooper muttered. "How are we going to get this over there before he leaves?"

The crowd was picking up, and it was getting more difficult to see Charles in the dust and sea of people. Cooper saw him lifting up a necklace exactly like he had in his visions, but he realized then that it was not the amulet he had around his neck.

"It should be there," he said frustratingly.

Suddenly, Billy let out an exceedingly long, strange sound of alarm wrapped in concern.

"Ummmmmmmmmm, Coop?"

Cooper was still watching what he could see of Charles. At least, he thought it was Charles.

Dammit!

"Coop," Billy repeated, "I don't think that it's the day after the battle after all."

"What?" Alyssa asked, looking at Billy mystified. "What do you mean?"

Billy was pointing at a grimy poster loosely affixed on a nearby wall.

"Unless…" Cooper continued in his own world, inhaling sharply before taking a step forward into the market.

"Unless what?" Charles Crosse suddenly said pointedly, stepping right in front of him.

Startled, Cooper took several tumbling steps back.

Alyssa's jaw was on the floor as she read the poster Billy had pointed out, at least the parts of it she could understand. "No… way…"

"You are really bad at spying on people young man," Charles said scornfully. His eyes seemed to pierce any attempt at resistance Cooper tossed out . "Now tell me: why is it you are so interested in me? Do I owe you or your bosses money?"

"Nothing like that at all," Cooper insisted. "Rather, I have something that you might be interested in, Charles. An artifact like the ones I know you like to collect."

"I… I don't know a Charles Crosse," he replied apprehensively. "The name's Landon. Landon Merryforth."

"No, it's Charles," Cooper replied, taking out the amulet, "and I never said anything about a last name, Mr. Crosse. The Order really does have trouble keeping all of its stories in line doesn't it?"

Alyssa and Billy staggered up behind Cooper, watching as Charles stared, transfixed at the silvery disc in front of him.

"No…" Charles said quietly. "That cannot be it! Can it?"

Cooper held it out a little bit further. "I'm not sure what 'it' means to you, but this thing… I thought it was meant for me but I'm told – by a higher authority – that it's meant for you."

A smile snuck onto Charles' face as he cautiously took the amulet into his cupped hands. "I have been looking for this for quite some time," he told Cooper, "and how strange that a wolf shifter and his two friends would bring it to me on the very day that I planned to give up searching for it."

"How very strange indeed," Cooper replied, realizing that Charles definitely knew his stuff relative to the supernatural.

Billy leaned in to whisper something. "Cooper, do you have any idea what day it is?"

"Yes," he answered. "The day we were meant to be here."

"Cooper, it's 2009!" Alyssa said loudly.

Charles was perplexed, the expression on his face a pretty obvious *no shit it's 2009 Sherlock,* but the amulet soon caught his attention again. "How much?" he asked.

"Oh about four freaking years," Billy scoffed.

"How much money?" Charles clarified.

"Nothing," said Cooper. "As I said earlier, it's meant for you, and…" Cooper paused, wanting to tell Charles so much more. He decided against it. "The only thing I ask is that you help get us home."

"After finding some clothes that fit," Billy insisted.

Charles laughed, looking from Billy to Alyssa, then Cooper. "Not sure I'm going to be putting any of this in my journal."

Cooper chuckled. "And that would be perfectly fine with me."

2

Thursday October 22, 2009

The trio fell in behind Charles as he led the way out of the bazaar.

"How are we going to get out of here and back to where we belong?" Alyssa asked.

"I don't know yet," Cooper replied, "but getting out of here with Charles' help is going to be the easy part. Getting back to *when* we belong is another matter. Let's hope that Charles, or someone else he knows might be able to help."

"Someone that's part of the Order?" Billy asked. "That doesn't freak me out one bit!"

Cooper smiled reassuringly. "That, my friends, is why I'm glad we're all still in this together." Saying that, Cooper drew his arms around both Alyssa and Billy and pulled them in close. "I love you guys!" Then he looked up, and saw that Charles had gotten well ahead of them. "Hey Charles, wait up! Geez, why do you have to walk so fast?"

3

Six Years Later

Saturday October 17, 2015

What started as a faint, white light grew to cover an entire square tile in the floor of a dank and musty cellar. The solid stone became like gravel, then dissolved further into powder. The tiny motes took on the muted shape of Solomon's third seal – a circular sigil used for protection against enemies and evil spirits lingering around one's home. Then, like a candle blown out atop a birthday cake, it vanished in billowing curls.

Well that did somethin' thought Gage Crosse as he cleared away the loose strands of dark hair that had fallen over his eyes. Dressed in a tight pair of jeans, boots, and nothing else, he had initially backed away, startled, but soon regained composure.

Gage peered into the alcove that had opened; it was barren, except for a mahogany jewelry box in the middle. Sitting on four small, clawed feet, it was adorned with golden floral patterns on each of its eight corners. The lid slowly rose by itself, revealing an amulet nestled in a wadded silk cloth that shimmered between ephemeral shades of blue and gray. Unknown to Gage, it had been waiting there ever since being given to his father by a young man named Cooper Bennett.

Gage reached out, unwilling (perhaps unable) to touch the plain metal surface. His hand quivered a hair's breath from the shiny disc before an overwhelming urge to set his fingers down drove him to do just that.

It's okay, Gage heard a young man's voice whisper. *You have to do this. Your destiny awaits…*

As his skin touched the cool metal, it sizzled, scalding pain surging straight up Gage's tattooed arm and into his head. Gruesome and prophetic visions shook his mind, forcibly commanding all of his senses…

***

…and when they were finished, Gage was left alone in the gloomy cellar with far too little breath. Lying in a heap on the floor, he worked to build his capacity back. Sitting up on his knees, he was still drawn to the spiky chain and round bit of silver that threatened to turn his life upside down. Gage grabbed hold of it, and lifted it over his neck.

The amulet came to rest on a rose tattoo that dominated the center of his chest. Feeling empowered, Gage stood up on his feet, giving the area a final once-over before heading back to the ladder to climb out. That's when he – like Cooper before – met his destiny proper, and his life was sent on a new path.

Placing a boot on the lowest rung, a rumble started in the ground, continuing to grow in strength with each subsequent step until Gage passed through some warded threshold his dad must have put in place.

When the amulet was carried past the ward's protections, the foundations of the house trembled at once. The talisman floated away from Gage's chest, pausing in mid-air. He spread his arms out for balance.

Without warning, vivid red spindles erupted from the pendant, spinning high into the late afternoon sky above the Denver home. They coalesced, the clouds themselves groaning and cracking under the onslaught. Forks of intense lightning careened down and out across countless miles, and everything that the violent bolts touched vaporized in bursts of shadow and flame. Then, as quickly as it all started, it was gone.

"What the hell was that?" Gage shouted, his country accent peppered with cumbersome gasps. "Getting' a lil' bit weirded out by the deadly laser beams shootin' out of this thing!"

There was a woman who met him at the top of the stairs, spectral and fair. "It was a signal," said Madeline Crosse coolly, and her son looked concerned.

Adrienne Elkins (Gage's Journeyman Field Operative partner-in-crime) had returned to his side, helping him out of the doorway. Also troubled, she turned to Madeline.

"A signal?" Ady asked. "To whom?"

"My dear," Madeline sighed, her ghostly form especially grave, "to everyone…"

<u>The Story Begins</u>

Find out what led to Cooper's trials and friendships in:

The Secret Life of Cooper Bennett by Golden Czermak.

Available in e-book, paperback, and audiobook formats.

***

<u>The Other Side of the Story</u>

Find out what happens to the Devil's Ire, the Journeymen, and the Great Demon Dajjal in:

The Journeyman Series by Golden Czermak.

Available in e-book, paperback, and audiobook formats.

Homeward Bound (Book 1)

Seal of Solomon (Book 2)

Made to Suffer (Book 3)

The Devil's Highway (Book 4)

Then Hell Followed (Book 5)

Running on Empty (Book 6)